D1149889

The Grace Church Mystery Series

DEATH IN THE OLD RECTORY

"I enjoyed *Death in the Old Rectory* so much that at times I found myself laughing out loud because each character brought personality to the story. I visualized the scenes as if watching a live performance where each character played their part extremely well. As Detective Joyce and Officer Chen, along with Lester (an unofficial security and criminal expert), begin to uncover the clues of the murder, the fun and adventure begin."
—Vernita Naylor for Readers' Favorite Reviews

DEATH IN THE MEMORIAL GARDEN

"Lovable characters, atmospheric charm, and sins from the past make this a must for brick & murder readers."
—Mary Daheim, author of the Bed-and-Breakfast Mysteries and the Alpine/Emma Lord Mysteries

"A heart-warming story filled with likeable characters as they deal with murder, mishaps, and mayhem. An insightful view into the challenges faced by today's urban churches. I look forward to the next murder at Grace Church."
—Liz Osborne, author of *Dirty Laundry*, A Robyn Kelly Mystery

"Deviny had a challenge on her hands and she met it and exceeded it. With her character development, her take on a subject that is divisive with the Church, and solid pacing I'm

looking forward to more installments with the other characters taking their turn in the spotlight. Recommended."
—Vikki Walton, I Love a Mystery

5 Stars: "This book is so good it practically reads itself. Let me tell you a secret. I was very tired as I read this, but this book was so exciting that I could not sleep! I did not nod off once. If you like mysteries, this book is for you. It is practically squeaky clean, and it is enjoyable reading for a winter's night."
—My Devotional Thoughts

"A fast-paced tale that has intrigue, mystery and humor all rolled up into a neat little story that takes place over a span of one week .... the storyline has surprising twist and turns coupled with satirical humor that will keep you engaged, and a quirky cast of characters who are a lot of fun."
—Jersey Girl Book Reviews

"I just loved following the day-to-day activities of this crazy group that is keeping Grace Church running on a wing and a prayer! Author Kathie Deviny does a great job creating three-dimensional characters, not only the aspects of them that play into the solving of the mystery but random miscellaneous traits that simply make them REAL."
—Words by Webb

"I did enjoy the casual nature of this story and it was short enough that I read it in one sitting. If you are looking for something to read while relaxing – this is the book. I give this book a 4 out of 5 stars."
—The Stuff of Success

"If you are a member of a small, older church, you will definitely relate to the characters of the altar guild, vestry and organist.... The book is humorous, satirical in the right

places and a lively little read. I highly recommend it for a light afternoon read!"
—Bless Their Hearts Mom

"A great cozy…. with a big mystery to solve and colorful characters. I look forward to reading her next book!"
—Book Lovers Stop

5 Stars: "I love a nice, cozy mystery! This novel had some wonderfully eccentric characters; Daniel the organist was my personal favorite. Set in an Episcopalian church, the mystery is reminiscent of Agatha Christie's 'Miss Marple' series, except this time, instead of villagers, we have church members. Very nicely done; I hope this is the first in a series."
—The Self-Taught Cook

"There were many revelations, twists and turns that I was not expecting. Deviny weaves a charming mystery that can be read in one sitting."
—Wanted Readers Blogspot

"A very light-hearted mystery, not too much depth involved with the characters or the location. I would definitely recommend this to all readers of cozy mysteries."
—A Date with a Book

"A fun and quick read. It makes me smile to reflect on it!"
—Beth Art from the Heart

"A fun, cozy mystery that combines two threads: a whodunit and a drive to save a valuable community resource …. A very quick read with characters who will capture your heart. It's the perfect way to spend an afternoon relaxing."
—Popcorn Reads

Death in the Old Rectory

Death in the Old Rectory

A Grace Church Mystery

~~~

KATHIE DEVINY

Seattle, WA

CAMEL PRESS

Camel Press
PO Box 70515
Seattle, WA 98127

For more information go to: www.camelpress.com
deviny.camelpress. com

Cover design by Sabrina Sun

Death in the Old Rectory
Copyright © 2016 by Kathie Deviny

ISBN: 978-1-60381-343-3 (Trade Paper)
ISBN: 978-1-60381-344-0 (eBook)

Library of Congress Control Number: 2015956057

Printed in the United States of America

Acknowledgments

~~~

C ATHERINE TREADGOLD, THE PUBLISHER of Camel Press, provided invaluable support and meticulous editing, and also her musical expertise and knowledge of the Episcopal Church. Jennifer McCord, associate publisher and executive editor, supplied necessary tough love to a writer who was rushing through her second manuscript. Hooray for Indie Publishers.

Thanks to Shelly Rotondo and Mike Regis of Seattle's Northwest Harvest for the good work they do and for answering many questions about food bank operations.

Thank also to Carol Webb, Don Holtz and the volunteers at the Trinity Thrift Shop. They taught me how to hang clothes correctly, sort and price donations, and which ones to throw in the free box. I had a wonderful time volunteering there.

I am fortunate to have as a friend and Seattle writing group member Joan Burton, author of *Best Hikes with Kids: Western Washington and the Cascades* (Mountaineers Books). She read the "almost final" draft of the manuscript and saved me from the disgrace of giving two names to the same person and having the same event happen on two different days, to name just two examples.

I'm proud of the accomplishments of the writing group's other members. Mary Will and Barbara Whyte Ray have written memoirs: *A Life Well Lived* and *Don't Push the River*. Cheri Tucker has published a novel about sorority life, *Hope Chest*. Cheri was also the one who informed me that people named Dominic were always referred to as Dom back in the day. Linda Lamb shared the skills learned in her national and local journalism career, and supports Hugo House, our local writing center. Linda also introduced me to Camel Press. Suzanne Rizzotti writes heartfelt essays about family life and children's education.

My writing group in Santa Barbara, especially Thelma Schmidhauser and Suzanne Ahn, keep me on the straight and narrow, asking for details, details, details.

People always wonder if a writer's characters are based on real persons. Not always, but I'm indebted to a handsome actor from the 1980s and a local California broadcaster for contributing to my portrayal of Nick. Daniel, Grace Church's organist, is inspired by an equally obsessed person from Seattle, but obsessed with a different subject. However, all of my characters are fictional.

Some of my family and friends will notice that I've included their first or last names in the character list, just for fun.

Blessings to you all, and, as always, to Paul.

Chapter One

~~~

THE BEGINNING OF THE end had been five months ago, a chilly, windswept April day.

"Father, a minute of your time?" Adele Evans stood in the doorway of the rector's office at Grace Church, Seattle, wearing a maroon version of the pants suit that was her uniform. Although no taller than 5'5", she was an imposing figure. She had excellent posture, and with the extra height of her gray French-twist, didn't appear much shorter than the balding rector when they stood side by side, despite his extra five inches of height. Mrs. Evans was the president of the Ladies' Auxiliary, directress of the Altar Guild, and the chair of many other committees.

She was also a frequent volunteer in the church office.

Father Robert Vickers, the rector of Seattle's Grace Parish church, had been enjoying a sardine sandwich and listening to the noon news. Because his mouth was full, he motioned her in. It wouldn't do to turn her away.

His visitor headed toward an armchair across the room, in order, he suspected, to put them on equal footing. Swallowing the last morsel of sandwich, he removed his feet from the desk, wiped his thick glasses with a stray tissue, and joined her in the seating area.

"How nice of you to give up your lunch hour to call on me, Mrs. Evans," he began. "See, I remembered you don't like the *Ms.* Prefix. I can't say that I blame you. *Mzzz* sounds like a buzz saw. Maybe someday you'll take up my offer to call me Father Robert, instead of Father Vickers, and then I can call you Adele. Don't you think Vickerzzz sounds like a buzz saw also?" He took a deep breath. "Now, how can I help you?" A counterattack was his only hope of slowing down the steamroller that was Adele Evans before it rolled right over him.

Mrs. Evans pointed over his shoulder to the empty sardine can on the desk and countered, "Be careful, Father, or you'll get grease all over your clerical collar. We Altar Guild ladies have enough to do without acting as a cleaning service."

She fixed him with a severe stare. "And you must say something to Deacon Mary. Last Sunday we discovered chocolate stains all over her white robe."

Father Robert quickly said, "Oh don't worry, my collar's plastic so I can remove any spots with powdered cleanser. Of course, it would be wonderful if the Altar Guild had the wherewithal to purchase linen collars, but I know you have much better uses for your funds. Why, those multicolored carnations were just the right touch at last Sunday's service."

Seeing that she was about to speak, he soldiered on, "Speaking of expenditures, I do have to put my foot down with regard to the altar candles. This was the second time they've burned out in the middle of the service. God's been generous to us at Grace Church, and I think the least we can do is replace the candles before they're down to nubs. I'm sure you agree."

She didn't agree; that was clear, so he went on, "Now, of course, Deacon Mary's robe isn't plastic. I will speak with her. Maybe the Sunday school children hugged her with their little chocolate-covered hands." Mrs. Evans' narrowed eyes said he'd gone too far. Deacon Mary's chocoholism was the worst-kept secret of the parish. He'd better let Adele have her say.

"Father, we have a much more important matter to discuss." Peering over the top of her reading glasses, she pinioned him with her eyes. "Now, I'm sure you haven't meant to be selfish in your use of the rectory provided you by the parish, but you must realize that it was built to house a large clerical family, not a single man."

Uh-oh. He wasn't sure if he could bluster his way out of this one. When Grace Church had called him as their rector six years ago, part of his compensation had included rent-free housing next door to the church. It was a common practice; his three previous parishes had also provided rectory housing. He'd often wondered where he'd end up after retirement.

Father Robert had tried to be generous with the space, often accommodating visiting clergy and boarding students in the extra bedrooms. Most recently, he'd provided lodging for the church's young organist Daniel, until Daniel had moved out to live with his father.

After Daniel left, Lester, the church's new night sexton, had moved into the second-floor bedroom. Robert still teared up remembering how Lester fell to his knees at the doorway, thanking God for ending twenty years of living on the streets.

That still left three drafty bedrooms and one and a half baths on the second floor unused, because Robert had remodeled the third floor attic for his quarters. The old fir walls and the splendid view of the city had proved irresistible. He held informal meetings and small receptions on the first floor, and he was a whiz in the kitchen, but his personal time was spent in the attic hideaway.

"So, Mrs. Evans," Robert said, "I'm sure you have something in mind. Whatever it is, you must know that the vestry will need to give its blessing."

"Certainly, Father," she parried. "I've made some preliminary inquiries and feel certain that the blessing will be forthcoming." Her lipstick-free lips twitched.

"And what exactly is your idea?"

Mrs. Evans picked up two presentation folders from the side table, handing one to him. The folder's title said it all: *The Grace Church Charity Thrift Shop and Community Outreach Office.* Even without having studied many business plans, he realized within a minute that what he was looking at would pass muster in a downtown-Seattle boardroom. She led him through the sections labeled *background, vision, mission statement, goals, deliverables, timelines* and *outcomes.*

Appendix A was a floor plan of the rectory with an overlay designating the living room for men's clothing, household items, and a cashier station. The dining room would be devoted to women's clothing and accessories and a dressing room.

The study, a holdover from the days when the rector had the luxury of studying before composing the Sunday sermon, would be used for sorting and pricing donations. The kitchen and adjacent half bath would be a break area for volunteers, who could use the sink to clean up the dirtier donations.

All but one of the second-floor bedrooms would be converted to offices for the church's food bank, located in the old gym behind the rectory. The staff were now perched precariously where the upstairs bleachers used to be. The remaining bedroom was labeled Thrift Shop Manager.

Father Robert couldn't sit still one minute longer. He rose from the chair and began pacing about, careful to avoid the papers piled on the floor, which served as his filing system.

"Very impressive, Mrs. Evans, especially the use of graphics." He picked up the folder and flipped through it. "Like this chart on page ten summarizing the need for the project, and the graph on page—let's see—twelve, showing community benefit. Oh my, I've never seen a graph go from zero to one hundred percent so quickly."

He gave her a long look. "In order to get all this data, you must have consulted with a few people. I assume you found the floor plans in the sexton's office, or maybe the archives. And you must have talked to Terry Buffett at the Food Bank. What was his reaction?"

Mrs. Evans took a water bottle from her purse and took a long drink before answering. "Oh no, Father, that would be your responsibility. However, as chairwoman of the parish outreach committee, I'm familiar with their operation and talk to Terry on a regular basis. I'm well aware that lack of office space hinders their ability to provide the optimal level of services."

"And Lucy Lawrence," he continued, "have you spoken to her?" Lucy was the senior warden, the chair of the church's vestry.

"I merely mentioned informally to her that a proposal might be forthcoming."

He wanted nothing more than to wrap this up. "So, Mrs. Evans, I can see how the parish rectory meets your criteria for size and location perfectly. But," he flipped through a few more pages, "don't proposals like this normally include at least two other options, if only to highlight the benefits of the preferred location?"

His attempt at a chuckle turned into a gargle. And his face was warm, never a good sign. Although he had several snide comments on the tip of his tongue, he was sick of hearing himself talk. The obvious question was, where would he move? But he already knew the answer, even before viewing Appendix B, which described his new digs in detail.

Pausing to make sure he was finished, and disregarding his question, Mrs. Evans said, "To summarize, Father, the conversion of the rectory for this purpose will—I mean, would—allow Grace Parish to provide the three necessities which our Lord preached about: feeding the hungry with the food bank, housing the needy at the halfway house across the street, and now clothing the naked at the Grace Parish Thrift Shop." She rested her case.

Father Robert sat down and tossed the proposal toward one

of the piles. "And for my summary, just let me say this: you make a persuasive case, very persuasive. You've almost persuaded me that leaving my lovely historic home conveniently located next to the church—the scene of many parish meetings and new member receptions, a home away from home for visiting students and pastors—is a no-brainer. *Almost.*" He cleared his throat. "Is that all, Mrs. Evans? Because if it is, I need to spend the afternoon in meditation and prayer."

"Of course, Father." She nodded toward him, much as a nun might to a priest.

"Just one more thought, if I may." Her head remained bowed. "I realize that the church-owned condo is somewhat bland. I can't help but think that Mrs. Ferguson would be the perfect person to help with decorating. She has such a flair, don't you think, and could help you make the space your very own."

Mrs. Ferguson was Molly, the love of his life, a widow who just last week had accepted his proposal of marriage. Although the news hadn't been made public yet, their relationship was no secret. He translated Mrs. Evans's comment to mean that having his own space would offer the necessary privacy for Molly and him to engage in … whatever they wanted to engage in.

Father Robert stayed seated as Adele left, in an inexcusable display of inhospitality. After the door closed, he took his cellphone from his pocket and texted Molly, *When you get a break, listen to the message I'm leaving on your cell.* The message he then left began, "I need you to come over and pull me off the ceiling," and continued with variations on the theme of "How dare she?" and "They're not getting rid of me so easily!"

Then Father Robert stood and looked through the large glass window that took up the top half of his office door. It had been installed at the direction of the church insurance company so that any impropriety on his part vis-à-vis a visitor could be seen and documented. The intention was good, but the result was that anyone in the outside office had to duck their heads to avoid witnessing such sights as prominent members of the church sobbing because of a financial or spiritual crisis.

Father Robert fast-walked through the office, telling Arlis, his afternoon secretary, "Food bank!"

Arlis, who had replaced Marion and also served as the food bank's bookkeeper, texted Terry the manager, *Father's headed your way and he's not happy.*

Terry didn't notice the text, because he was engaged in shooting hoops with Nick, one of the food bank volunteers. They made quite a pair—Nick big and burly, Terry short and slender. Because they were standing upstairs in the old bleacher area, their shots fell down toward the one hoop remaining from the old gym. Mel, another volunteer stationed below, lobbed the ball back up. The three switched positions every ten minutes. They'd get back to work as soon as the afternoon food distribution began.

Father Robert came up behind Terry and Nick, having entered from an access door located off the Sunday school rooms.

"Why didn't you tell me? I thought you were my friend!"

Terry jumped. Nick yelled "Holy Crap!"

The three faced off for a minute, and then Terry said, "I was afraid to."

"What are you talking about?" asked Nick.

Terry said, "See you later, bro." Nick saluted and left.

It took an hour and two beers at a tavern down the street for Robert and Terry to reconcile. Terry admitted that he lusted for decent office space and had convinced himself that Robert would be happy to move to the condo. Robert steamed and stewed for a while, but decided their friendship took precedence over his ego.

Because of the beers, Father Robert took the rest of the afternoon off, and at five called his senior warden, Lucy Lawrence.

"Why didn't I know about this plan of Adele's?" he asked, a bit too loudly.

Lucy answered, "She mentioned her proposal to me on Sunday, and I told her not to say another word until she'd talked to you. And that the vestry would only consider the idea if you proposed it yourself. Now, why didn't I warn you then?"

"I don't know, Lucy, why?"

There was a pause as Lucy deliberated over her answer. "Father, I don't think you realize how many people approach me each week with wonderful ideas for making Grace Church the premier house of God in the United States. I guess I've gotten into a wait and see habit. But I should have known better than to dismiss Adele in the same way. I'm sorry that you were blindsided and will do anything in my power to resolve this."

"Thank you, Lucy, that's all I can ask." Ordinarily he would have continued the conversation, but Father Robert was anxious to consult with Molly, who had invited him to dinner.

AN HOUR LATER, SEATED at her oval Danish Modern dining table, he let loose. "Molly, I hate this. I hate being challenged this way. I know that when we're married I'll be living in this wonderful home with you. But until then I can't stand the thought of being exiled to a cookie cutter condo in a building full of young urban professionals on the make."

With a broad smile that lit up her amber eyes, Molly replied, "I imagine that at least a few are older retired professionals enjoying life to the fullest." He so admired Molly's serenity in the face of a crisis. And now, as always, he took in her curvy figure and the curly auburn hair that framed her heart-shaped face and wondered how an average-looking Joe like him had gotten so lucky.

"You're right, sweetheart, that's not it. It's … it's … let me think while I devour this chicken pot pie."

"Lovingly provided by our local Foodie Market," she said.

After further discussion, they agreed that Robert felt as though no one appreciated how his presence in the rectory had benefited the parish for all the years he'd been single. He'd made himself indispensable, to the point of running next door in the middle of the night every time the old-fashioned alarm sounded, so as to avoid a fine from the fire department. And to the point of welcoming parishioners at all hours, no matter how insignificant their issue, and answering the knock on the door from anyone looking for a handout.

Over a Foodie Market dessert of pear tart with *crème fraiche*, he said, "I hate the idea of moving. The problem is, it makes so much sense. On the other hand, I'm convinced that this is a power play on Adele's part."

"You know, Robert, you're probably right on both counts," Molly said.

THE VESTRY MET THE next Sunday after services. This was one of the few years Mrs. Evans wasn't on the vestry, but she was sitting quietly in the corner of the meeting room in case there were questions.

There were questions, none that Father Robert hadn't asked himself. Mrs. Evans answered clearly and concisely, which pleased the vestry members who wanted to get home before the start of the Seahawks game.

Given his turn, Father Robert stopped short of a hearty endorsement but refused to offer a rebuttal, despite urging from Lucy Lawrence. The vestry voted their approval six to two.

Chapter Two

~~~

A MOVING VAN ARRIVED at the rectory door on a sunny day in late June. Father Robert and most of his belongings were transported five blocks north to the fourth floor of the Vistaview Condominiums. Unit 403 was part of a recent bequest from parishioners Neola and Fred Peterson, the remainder of which was being used to repair the church's crumbling bell tower.

The Petersons had bought the condo eight years ago for their recently divorced adult daughter and her two children. But Audrey had much preferred the suburbs and was soon remarried to someone who felt the same way.

The events surrounding her mother's funeral had only strengthened Audrey's resolve to live the rest of her life outside the Seattle city limits, and she'd gladly signed away any claim to the property.

Six weeks after Robert was removed from the rectory, its first floor was open for business as Grace Thrift Shop. Whatever else he thought of Mrs. Evans, Robert had to admire her organizational skills. She'd recruited and trained volunteers from both Grace Parish and the nearby Baptist church. The local retirement homes had deluged them with donations, and their residents had solicited toys and books from their grandchildren.

Parishioners dropped off things on their way into Sunday services. When a parolee from the church-sponsored halfway house graduated to freedom or was demoted back to prison, any unclaimed items were sent across the street to the shop. Most of the baseball caps and electronic gadgets came in that way.

Sadly, the beautiful tiled fireplace where Robert and Molly had toasted marshmallows on their first date was now blocked by a display shelf. The large city-view windows were covered over with curtains for sale and macramé plant holders, mobiles, and wall hangings.

ON THIS DRIZZLY MONDAY morning in October, Robert stared out his living-room window. The "vista view" from his condo was the bare wall of the hospital's surgical tower. If he jammed the side of his face to the hermetically sealed glass and rotated to the left, he could see a few inches of Puget Sound between two other towers. If he tilted his neck down, he could see the tops of three maple trees. They formed bright red circles at this time of year, which were pretty, but left his other senses with nothing to do. If only he could open the window to hear something other than the whoosh of the condo's air handling system. It would be heavenly if he could feel the breeze. Most of all, he'd like to smell the aroma wafting from the pizza place on the corner.

He was bored. Bored and lonely. Monday was his day off. Since yesterday's services, he'd had no funerals or meetings or anything else to interfere with twenty-four hours straight of nothing to do. For Robert, this kind of inaction was like a prison sentence. An extrovert, he needed to be around other people to be happy.

The love of his life, Molly, was two miles away at her unpaid job as the bishop's secretary. Because Molly's father, now deceased, was also a bishop, it seemed a natural position for her, especially since her late husband had left her a wealthy woman who didn't need to work to support herself. The only day off he and Molly shared, Saturday, he'd been busy performing a wedding and attending an ordination. Last night she'd hosted visiting relatives, so tonight couldn't come soon enough.

They'd gotten to know each other last spring when Grace Church was the scene of a mysterious death. That had drawn the bishop's attention and he'd designated Molly, a recent widow and dedicated churchwoman, as his emissary to the parish. Robert had fallen under the spell of her mature beauty and was bolstered by her support as his world fell around him in the aftermath of the tragic event. The happiest day of his life was when she'd accepted his marriage proposal.

After the mystery was solved, Molly started attending Grace church, and had won over everyone who might have objected to their relationship. She'd volunteered for unpopular tasks, so that no one would feel she was trying to take over. She didn't gossip, and gracefully deflected all efforts to communicate with Father indirectly through her.

Wonderful as she was, Molly would not be happy if he called just to pass the time, and the bishop would be downright grouchy. For now, maybe he could sneak into the attic of the old rectory.

If events proceeded as planned, he and Molly would be sharing her lovely Northwest Modern home located just three miles away next to a greenbelt, so he'd left his books and his *Mad* magazine collection in their custom-built shelves in the rectory's attic bedroom. People said that his hobby of collecting a juvenile humor magazine popular in the 1960s was strange for a man of God in his mid-fifties. However, he reminded them, they often complimented him on his quirky sense of humor, which he attributed to the thousands of hours spent with Alfred E. Newman and friends.

Darn, he thought, the attic was off limits right now. The second-floor bedroom assigned to Lester Jones was now an office, so Lester had moved up to Robert's former quarters. He'd be asleep now, since he worked nights. Old Henry, the church's longtime sexton, finally agreed to delegate his janitorial duties, which were best done off-hours. Lester also made sure the grounds were secure after evening AA meetings, choir rehearsals, and the like.

Those leery of someone with Lester's non-existent résumé working at the church had been won over by the support he'd provided after the death last spring in the memorial garden. He also stayed up late to provide nice strong coffee for Sunday services, and ran an informal valet service to the parking area one block away. The tips the reformed panhandler received satisfied the handout habit he'd had trouble shaking.

Those same church members had even come to love his street dog, a German shepherd named Spike, who shared Lester's quarters at the old rectory. Robert hoped that Stacy Chase, the church's volunteer event organizer and publicist, had dropped her idea that Lester's rags-to-riches story would make a great film project and garner wonderful publicity.

Now he was not only bored and lonely, but hungry. And nervous. He had an appointment with the bishop next week to ask formal permission to marry Molly. He was lucky that his beloved knew about the feudal ways of the church. He couldn't imagine many other women who would allow their fiancée's boss to have the final say. His first wife certainly wouldn't have. And since there had been many other ways of the church she didn't approve of, that marriage was over about the same time he graduated from seminary. Fortunately, unlike the Catholic Church, the Episcopal Church allowed for remarriage in the church after divorce.

Because he was divorced, the bishop would have a whole list of things to grill him on: were alimony payments draining his salary? Would he love and leave Molly, whom the Bishop regarded as one might a valuable porcelain doll? And most importantly, would he be the cause of Molly resigning her volunteer position as the bishop's secretary? He dreaded the audience. The bishop would be interviewing Molly separately; would he try to talk her out of marrying someone well below her social status? He'd better spend a few minutes jotting down a list of rebuttals.

Chapter Three

~~~

.

As Father Robert worked on his list, the Seattle Metro bus route originating in the southeast portion of the city—the route that consistently won the weekday ridership sweepstakes—was beginning its 8:30 a.m. run. Five minutes after the first pickup point, people were hanging onto straps up and down the aisle, even though the morning commute had mostly ended.

This same route came in dead last in the on-time statistics, because it stopped at two hospitals. Many of its riders depended on wheelchairs and walkers for mobility and needed help getting on and off. It took a full minute for the driver to lower and raise the platform and make sure the rider was securely seated.

Drivers either loved or hated this run. The more extroverted relished the bustle, and prided themselves on their ability to defuse the little spats a crowded bus produces. The more introverted drivers, the ones who refused to call out the stops and grunted when wished a good day, longed for enough seniority to bid for another run.

One of the regular riders came up with the route's nickname

after being reprimanded by an introverted driver for talking too loudly with her seat mates. She and her compatriots were making their weekly visit to the mental health clinic at the public hospital.

"You'd better find another bus to drive, mister. Don't you know, this here's the nut run?"

This same Monday morning in early October, at 8:55 more or less, the nut run arrived at the public hospital stop, which also served a high rise public housing complex as well as the city's largest food bank, located in the old gym of Grace Parish Church. The doors had barely flapped open when a sizable contingent of passengers rushed headlong down the steps, ignoring their disabled fellows who had exiting priority.

The group darted in front of the bus and across three lanes of traffic toward the old stone church on the opposite corner. They pushed walkers, carry carts, and strollers. A portion peeled off at the church gate; the rest joined a line that stretched around the corner and down the hill toward the freeway.

At the stroke of nine the church doors opened, as did the sliding gate to the food bank around the corner. Both lines surged ahead, and then began moving slowly toward their goals: a voucher for the church thrift shop at the parish office and a bagful of groceries at the food bank.

The neighborhood around them was bustling too. Residents of another high rise, an upscale retirement complex, walked their terriers and pugs, stopping to visit with one another on the street-side benches. Parolees from the church-sponsored halfway house picked up litter and swept the sidewalk. Pedestrian commuters walked down the hill and under the freeway to their downtown offices. None of these activities was curtailed by the drizzle. It would take a tsunami for that to happen in the Pacific Northwest.

At 9:45 a woman and a man arrived at the thrift shop from opposite directions. Their volunteer shift started at 10. Mae Perkins made the one block journey from the public housing tower where she'd lived for twenty years. She wore a navy-blue wool coat against the chill. Its shiny gold buttons were embossed with tiny anchors, except for one dull gold replacement on the left wrist. She moved carefully through the maple leaves smeared along the sidewalk. What was obviously a blue-black wig sat atop her head. Mae claimed to be eighty-eight, but was really ninety-one. Her baptismal record was on file at Grace Church, which she'd attended since her baptism at the age of two months, but since hers was the longest membership, who was to know?

The man, in his forties—forty-five to be exact—arrived from the north, where he lived in a studio apartment above a dry cleaner. Dominic Monte, known to everyone as Nick, glided in on a bike. It was a sturdy bike, because he was built more like a linebacker than a Tour de France competitor. He wore a hooded Seattle Sounders sweatshirt and plaid Bermuda shorts, which revealed the thick dark hair of his muscular legs.

By this time, the church office had handed out most of the thrift shop vouchers, and the line had re-formed outside the yellow-shingled old rectory. The tall man and tiny woman maneuvered their way to the front of the line, ignoring the frowns and protests.

"You'll have nowhere to spend those vouchers if we can't unlock this front door," said Mae. "Nick, you stand guard here until I get behind the counter,"

"Yes, ma'am," saluted Nick. Turning to the line, he winked and said, "You treat her nice, now. She's my little sister." Laughter erupted, and continued for a few minutes as his comment was translated into a variety of languages.

Two hours later, there was a lull after Nick and Mae finished serving the first rush of customers.

"There go the last pair of men's pants," said Mae. "I'm going to call Martha at the retirement home. She'll get the ladies to go through their husbands' closets and pull some for us." She looked up. "Oh, hello, Dr. Lucy. I didn't see you come in."

Lucy Lawrence placed a bulging plastic sack on the counter. She was dressed in a parka and jeans. Her gray hair split on either side of her ears, as it tended to do when it drizzled.

"I've brought a new supply of toothbrushes—the kind with the toothpaste built in. The dental clinic gets them from the company that supplies the county jail. Don't forget to give them out each time you ring up a sale." Besides serving as senior warden, the retired dentist volunteered not only at the thrift shop but at the free dental clinic downtown. Her passion for oral hygiene knew no bounds.

"Thank God, Dr. Lucy!" Nick said. "My teeth are scummy." He removed a sample from the bag, tore off the covering and preceded to dry-brush his teeth, simultaneously instructing the five customers in the shop on proper procedure. "Wup 'n dn 'nd don' f'geph the chuing surfasss."

Mae and Lucy laughed; the customers smiled and shook their heads. Mae and Nick had heard a more professional version of this lecture many times when Dr. Lucy was on duty at the cash register. They hoped she didn't realize how many of her brushes were dropped into the shop's free box near the front door.

"Hey, bro!" Nick pulled the brush out and hailed Terry Buffett, who was coming down the stairs from his new office on the second floor. The food bank manager was dressed today all in black, except for a turquoise-studded bolo tie around the neck of his Western-style shirt. He wore his light brown hair in a crew cut and looked younger than his forty years.

He replied to Nick, "Hey, bro, that's my Hawaiian shirt you're wearing!" In order to approach the counter, he had to swerve around a clothes rack standing in the middle of the entry vestibule.

Nick threw up his hands. "You donated it, remember? After starting that crazy diet and losing all that weight you didn't need to lose. But," he continued, "if you want it that bad ...." He began unbuttoning the multicolored shirt decorated with Pelicans, revealing a hairy chest.

"Nick, stop!" both Mae and Lucy exclaimed. This time the customers laughed out loud. The bit with the toothbrush had just been a warm-up. Now Nick was about to go into a full-blown routine. Many people came to the shop when Nick was working just to watch his antics. Like when he'd ring up a new customer with a fifty-cent paperback and say, "That'll be twenty dollars." Or when he made a customer take away three donated videocassettes—the kind that no one played anymore.

Sometimes Mrs. Evans, the store manager, would come down from her office during a performance and things would rise to a new level of hilarity as Nick delivered one-liners in response to her scolding.

Mrs. Evans: "Nick, why isn't that mannequin dressed?"

Nick, wriggling his eyebrows: "Her outfit was frumpy. I like her better naked."

Mrs. Evans: "Where did these boxes of adult diapers come from?"

Nick: "From dead people. You may not have noticed, but the retirement tower over there has a nursing center hidden in it. I call it the last stop on the continuing care highway. And it's convenient for the families to dispose of the deceased's effects right here. We price the diapers at a dollar a box and they sell like hotcakes."

Even the customers knew that Mrs. Evans would never fire him. For one thing he was a volunteer—one of the few volunteers who could operate the shop's old-fashioned cash register. Mae, for instance, wouldn't go near the thing, preferring to tidy up the clothes racks and bag the purchases.

Everyone wondered about Nick's background. He'd appeared six months earlier and never mentioned a job or other means of support. He lived frugally in a studio nearby and bragged that all his belongings came from thrift shops. He got permission from Father Robert to wash and iron his clothes in the rectory basement. He volunteered for the food bank as well as the thrift shop and spent much of his down time in the rectory kitchen reading the donated textbooks and *National Geographic* magazines no one wanted to buy.

"As I was saying," Nick continued, "this shirt wouldn't fit you anymore, Terry; you're starting to look like a skeleton."

Terry had joined other food bank managers from the area in living for a month on the allocation provided to a typical food stamp recipient. He patted his nonexistent belly. "Man, this food stamp budget is kickin' my butt! A hundred bucks a month barely keeps me in coffee. It's gotten us some great publicity, though. Did you see the piece on KORN news showing me scrounging in the food bank remainder bins?"

"I've got it!" said Nick. "You write a diet book and call it the *Food Bank Fast*. That'll land you on Oprah before you can say 'I'm starving.'"

"Here, Terry, have a mint." Mae handed him a candy from the bowl on the counter.

"But brush your teeth afterward," said Lucy.

Chapter Four

~~~

EVERYONE LOOKED UP AS the clothes rack swayed, its hangers jangled, and the words "Goddamn it!" rose in the air. Terry turned around and waded into the jumbled pile of clothes to assist whoever was trapped there.

"Mr. Grafton, sorry about this. Everyone, this is Ed Grafton, our new board member. He's the owner of Grafton Transport. Ed, meet Nick, Mae, and Lucy, volunteers at the church's Thrift Shop."

Mr. Grafton stared at the group standing around the counter. They stared back. No one spoke.

"I guess we'd better go upstairs, Ed," Terry said. "Don't forget about the hockey game tomorrow," he called back to Nick.

"What are you doing having your headquarters at a dump like this?" Ed Grafton said, as they climbed the stairs. "I'll find some decent space for you."

"It a good thing he never saw Terry's office in the old gym," Mae said when they were out of earshot.

"Yeah," Nick said. "And I guess we'd better move that rack."

"Uh, Mr. Nick?"

"Hey, little guy, how's it going?" Nick said to Daniel, the

church's organist, who had just arrived and was going through the CD rack. Like Terry, Daniel looked younger than his twenty-five years. His short, skinny body, curly, dark brown hair and big brown eyes evoked everyone's protective instincts.

In a resonant voice too big for his body, Daniel said, "Well, I'm okay, I guess, except that I can't think of the right anthem for the choir to sing when we bless the animals in two Sundays. Father has moved the readings for St. Francis Day, which comes in the middle of the week, to that Sunday, so I can't refer to the lectionary to figure out the theme for the music. For instance, last Sunday was the fourteenth Sunday after Pentecost and the lessons all talked about Jesus feeding the multitudes so it was easy to decide that 'Feed my Sheep' would be a good anthem.

"Of course," he continued, "there are some other anthems that talk about animals, including one with words by St. Francis himself, called 'All Creatures of our God and King,' which is number four hundred in the hymnal. The problem is I already used it this year, for the Earth Day service we had in May."

"Dear, what are you talking about?" asked Lucy.

"I'm sorry to be confusing, Dr. Lucy. Let's just say I'm here searching for inspiration," Daniel said. "Did you know the animals are going to be in the church for the blessing? It was Ms. Stacy's idea; she's invited the newspapers to come and watch. The animal owners will lead their pets up to the altar rail, dogs first, and then the cats, and then everything else. Except that Father Robert said under no circumstances is he blessing a snake, even if it's in a cage. I guess I'll have to choose music that animals will like, too. Maybe Mr. Lester will let me borrow Spike so I can try some hymns out on him."

"Is that a Mahalia Jackson CD you've got in your hand?" Nick asked. "Bring it over. She's my favorite. Did you ever hear her sing in person, Mae?"

Mae rolled her eyes. "Oh yes indeed, she invited all two million of us old Black ladies to a special concert just before she died."

Nick staggered back, clutching his heart. "Got me," he told her, and then studied the back of the CD. "Here's an animal song for you, Daniel. 'His Eye is on the Sparrow.' He inserted the disk into the CD player next to the cash register. Mahalia's voice soared over the room:

> Why should I feel discouraged, why should the shadows come,
> Why should my heart be lonely, and long for heav'n and home.
> When Jesus is my portion? My constant Friend is He:
> His eye is on the sparrow, and I know He watches me;
> His eye is on the sparrow, and I know He watches me.
> I sing because I'm happy, I sing because I'm free,
> For His eye is on the sparrow, and I know He watches me.

Mae sighed. "That's taken from Matthew 10. It was sung at every funeral I attended with my mama. Not so much anymore. It's said that the sparrow takes the souls who have died to heaven."

"Daniel, can you make a note that I'd like this one played at my funeral?"

"Sure, Mr. Nick. I have lots of notes about funeral preferences. But wait … I know you're older than me, but not old enough to be planning your funeral. Unless of course you're very forward thinking, in which case I can file away your instructions for whoever comes after me, in the event I end up working somewhere else, not that I want to, of course."

Nick looked off to one side. "I guess you could say I'm forward thinking, Daniel. You just never know."

Mae said, "Daniel, you don't have to worry about your job here since you found out who killed Ms. Clare last spring." The four reminisced about that eventful time until the noon rush of lunch-hour shoppers arrived.

At one p.m., Stacy Chase, the church's self-appointed event coordinator, came in looking for serving plates to use at the sumptuous Sunday coffee-hour receptions she'd inaugurated a few months ago. Church attendance had climbed, although it was true that some of the new people merely waved at the sanctuary on their way to the parish hall, its tables laden with coffee, tea, pastries, and fruit.

The parish vestry, at her urging, had added a marketing category to the annual budget, on the condition that the line item would remain at zero until and unless Stacy found a way to fund it. She'd done so with a vengeance, to the point of a kerfuffle with Terry over which program—coffee hour or food bank—got the day-old pastries from the neighborhood Starbucks. She was now one of Terry's best food and cash solicitors, and they divided their spoils equitably.

Stacy's clothes did not come from a thrift store. Her teal blue sweater, accented with an Indian print scarf, black leggings, and tall black boots, were exactly right for early October. They suited her tall, slim frame and her highlighted honey-colored hair. She was protected from universal envy by her generous nature, a laugh that sounded like a seal's bark, and a chronically red nose.

Stacy's family, the Uptons, had attended Grace Parish for generations, so she and Rick had chosen the church for their wedding a year ago. Rick was a real estate developer who'd been drawn into a colleague's scheme to develop Grace church right off its property. After feeling the full force of Stacy and Father Robert's wrath, he was now on board and managing the restoration of the church tower.

"Mae, could you let me into the sorting room?" Stacy asked. "I want to see if there are any more of these dishes in there. She held up a vintage rectangular plate of ridged glass divided into three parts. "See? One of the sections holds this matching cup, and there are two for food. How cute is that?"

"Now, Ms. Stacy, you know Mrs. Evans wouldn't like you

going in there. As a matter of fact, the last time I let you in, she found out and took away my key. I think she's up in her office if you want to ask her in person."

Nick glanced at the plates and then launched into a sales pitch. "Excuse me ma'am, but the third section has a different function. Notice the indentation in the outside corner, which allows the ladies to park their cigarettes while eating cookies and drinking tea. There's enough room in that section for two, or maybe three extra butts. I would say that these plates are iconic, and of the highest standard for their time."

Stacey barked her seal-laugh. "You're priceless, Nick. I guess I'll pass, but why don't you post them on eBay? I'll bet the shop could get a hundred dollars for the set."

"Because Mrs. Evans feels that the thrift shop doesn't need the Internet," Nick said, "or the cordless phone or the electronic cash register. We rely on donations, and donors so far have only parted with their oldest technology." He continued, "And even if Bill Gates walked in with a new networked system, I'll bet she'd turn him down. She'd say that selling online and using PayPal would distract us from our humanitarian mission. The fact is, she's scared of technology."

Mae added, "It was a real effort to get her to agree to a microwave in the kitchen. We had to wait for a donation for that, too."

"Got it," said Stacy. "I'll put 'updating technology' on my to-do list. I'm sure we have some parishioners who are upgrading their computer equipment and would be glad to install it. And by the way, have you heard about the St. Francis' Day service coming up in two Sundays? Father Robert is letting the animals in the church, and I've contacted—"

"Yes, we've heard," they interrupted in unison.

"Okay, make sure to come. I guess I will go upstairs and butter up—bark, bark—I mean *visit* Mrs. Evans. She sees me as a threat to her power-lock on parish events, and I don't blame her. My strategy is to kill her with kindness, as it were. I'll tell her what a good job she's done curating the display of dishes."

"Perfect," said Nick.

"You go, girl," said Mae.

Stacy reached the foot of the stairs, still talking. "She's obviously never heard of succession planning, and I'm not going there with her, but she has to realize that at her age the reins of power start pulling away from you, like it or not."

"Got it," said Nick.

Stacy had reached the first landing but her musk scent lingered.

"Mrs. Evans will see through that in half a second," whispered Mae.

From the second landing, Stacy called back, "Mae, honey, don't forget to let me know if any size-eight designer dresses come in with the tags still on. I'm looking for an outfit to wear to the City Club benefit."

"Yes, ma'am," Mae called out.

To Nick, she whispered, "Honey, my patootie. The only way I'd know a designer dress would be if it bit me with its price tag."

"Come on, Mae, don't 'dis yourself like that. You're a flashy dresser. Look at that coat you wore in today. That's wool cashmere. So what if it came from here and was missing a button?"

Business had slowed again, and they passed the time discussing the interesting donations that came into the shop— things like used dentures and pornography among the book donations. Ed Grafton, the new food bank board member, came down the stairs and gave them a glare before exiting. A man came in and knelt in front of the free box, tossing items right and left. He got up to leave.

"Oh, no you don't!" said Mae. "Put all those things back the way you found them. What are you looking for anyway?"

"Some socks, ma'am," he muttered, tossing everything back in.

"All you needed to do was ask," said Mae. "Here's some new socks, and underwear too." After the man left, she went to the kitchen to make a cup of tea.

When she came back, Nick said, "I need a break. Hold the fort, *honey*." Mae picked up a can of air freshener and sprayed it at his departing back.

Chapter Five

~~~

FIFTEEN MINUTES LATER, THE sound of click, click, and click came from the stairway, heralding the appearance of a German shepherd dog, who arfed to Mae and then ambled over to the box containing animal toys and leashes. Most had been donated by bereaved pet owners.

"Any of you in here allergic to dogs?" Mae called out. When no one replied, she said, "Okay, Spike, you can stay. You know, dog, every time I say your name, I think of the dog named Spike on the old Buster Brown radio show. Of course, no one remembers that now."

"Hey, Spike, don't even try to fit into that sweater," Nick said, returning from break. "It came from a Havanese."

" 'Bout time you got back," Mae said. Look at this line of folks waiting to check out."

Spike sniffed at the donated food bowls, played a minute with a rope toy, and then wandered around the store greeting the shoppers. A few minutes later, heavy footsteps sounded on the stairs and Lester, Spike's owner, appeared.

"Hello, *compadres.* Spike, give the pacifier back to that baby!"

"Lester!" said Nick and Mae in unison.

"Man, I am whupped," Lester said. "I'm not used to bedding down on a mattress. I'll have to look for a board to put over it, so's I can get some decent sleep. Come on, you lazy dog, time to make the rounds of the pre-rim-ter and find old Henry, so he can yell at me about all the chores I haven't done."

"Twenty minutes to closing," Nick said at 2:40. "Let's start the checklist." The few remaining shoppers perked up for a final performance.

"Books in alphabetical order?"

"Check."

"Dressing room empty?"

"You told me you wanted that job, 'cause mostly it's ladies who use it."

Lester re-entered the shop. He pointed up the stairs and Spike ascended. Then he called out to the two remaining customers, "Sorry, folks, you got to leave early today." One look at Lester, who was holding a shovel he'd brought in from outside, and they left.

"What's up?" Nick asked.

"You tell me," answered Lester. "I'm wondering why Al, the guy who hangs out down the hill, has it in for you." Lester broadly defined the church perimeter to include his old buddies who congregated two blocks down at the freeway.

Seeing the expression on Nick's face, Lester moved closer to the counter. "Man, you look like you just got sucker-punched!"

Mae, too, moved closer. "Here, sit down."

Nick answered, "No, I'm fine. Al? Has it in for me? What did he say, Les?"

"He didn't. He just asked if you were working today. I told him yeah, what was it to him, and he just nodded. So I told him he'd better stay cool or he'd be dealing with me and you together."

Mae reached up and tapped Nick on the shoulder. "Remember, a few weeks ago you made him and another guy leave 'cause they were arguing and pushing at each other. You picked up the phone like you were going to call the police."

The breath that Nick took strained the buttons of Terry's Hawaiian shirt. "That's it? That's all it is?"

Lester held his ground two feet away from Nick. "Like I said, you tell me."

"I guess he thought I gave him the evil eye, or something. He must be used to being run out of places, with that mouth of his."

Lester said, "You gotta watch him a little bit more than the others around here. He's strong enough and mean to boot. Spike growls when he sees him. Keep an eye open, brother."

AT 2:55, ADELE EVANS came down the stairs from her office, dressed in a denim pants suit and white sneakers. Her gray hair was in its usual French twist, and her stern aspect was somehow made more so by the scarlet frames of her glasses.

She scanned the shop. Everything was tidy, as she liked it. Mae was rehanging women's clothes on their racks. Nick was bent over the counter tallying the day's proceeds.

"What was the take?" she asked.

Nick jumped. "Ahhhhh! Don't *do* that, Adele!"

"Nick, you know I don't like being referred to by my first name."

"If you don't want to be called Adele, then don't call me Nick. What was the take? What would you say if I told you a jewelry buyer spotted a diamond ring in the locked case. And that he offered two grand and I bargained him up to five?"

Mae called from the next room, "And that we had to call Officer Chen working food bank security to take the check to the bank."

Mrs. Evans turned on a silent heel and marched out the front door, slamming it behind her.

"Oooh EEE!" said Mae. "You're in big trouble now."

"What's she going to do, fire me? Actually, we did pretty

well—about two hundred in vouchers and one hundred cash." He looked at the front door. "I should treat her better, given the good she's doing. I just don't get why she has to be so smug about it."

Mae patted down the last of the plastic bags she was folding. The shop received ten donated bags for one salable donation. "Well, this church is about all she's got since her husband died. And her children don't come around much; they probably don't like her personality either."

At 3 p.m. sharp, Nick and Mae shooed the last customers out of the shop—the ones who'd snuck back in after Lester and his shovel left. Mae brought in the sandwich board from out front and locked the door, while Nick tidied up the counter. Then she went into the kitchen to empty the coffee pot and use the adjacent facilities.

Nick was putting loose change into an envelope when a voice said, "Long time no see, Dom."

Nick didn't jump this time, just looked up and said, "That's been fine with me."

"So long, Dom."

The last thing Nick saw was the gun pointed at his head and the familiar face behind it.

Chapter Six

"YOU DONE YET, NICK?" Mae said, coming back into the shop. "I've got an appointment to get my wig set. Now why is that front door open after I just locked it?"

She turned to the counter and squinted through her drugstore eyeglasses as she walked forward. "Nick, what are you doing behind there?"

When she saw his crumpled body, and the wound at the back of his head, she knew he was dead. She opened her mouth to scream, and feeling the light-headedness preceding a faint, told herself, *Oh no, you don't. You take a breath instead and tend to your friend.*

She walked around the counter, averting her eyes so she couldn't see where the back of his head had been. Nick's torso was slightly turned in her direction, so she checked for a pulse at his wrist, then at his neck, and saw the entry wound in his forehead. She noted how small it was, and that there was hardly any blood—there. She moved in close, and after touching the cross hanging from its chain—the one he always wore—she buttoned the Hawaiian shirt with the pelicans back up to a respectable second hole.

The old-fashioned phone attached to the wall was behind him, too far for her to reach. She kissed his cheek, not caring what the police would think, and walked to the stairs. She climbed them slowly and called 911 from the Food Bank office.

HAVING JUST RETURNED TO the condo from a lonely walk, Robert turned on the radio to listen to the news and idly heard the sirens approaching from the north. His unit faced a busy street in between two hospitals and near the freeway, so he barely paid attention. The sirens sounded much louder at the church because it was so near the county hospital and trauma center, and the tall stained-glass windows hadn't been designed with soundproofing in mind. When sirens yowled during the sermon or communion service, he would pause mid-sentence while his organist Daniel played a musical interlude. There were many interludes on cold Sunday mornings when the banging of the steam radiators added to the cacophony.

Today the aid car turned south at his corner and he pricked up his ears. They were heading in the direction of the church. At seven seconds exactly the sirens stopped. That was too soon for the public hospital. They had either stopped at the church or the halfway house across the street. He hesitated five seconds before deciding to check it out. He had nothing better to do.

And he might as well get some more exercise while he was at it. If all went as planned, and he and Molly were married within the next year, Robert wanted to fit into his best dark suit. Instead of taking the elevator, he ran down the condo's emergency stairs and out the side door, barely missing Mr. Blevins and his beagle Harry from 10C. Maybe someday he'd be able to run all five blocks to the church, but he paused after two, took three deep slow breaths, and then speed-walked the rest of the way.

Police and aid cars filled the street in front of the old rectory. The food bank line snaked around the crews on the sidewalk, undeterred despite the best efforts of the officers to disband it.

"I'm the pastor here. Let me in, please." He'd learned not to say the foreign words *priest* or *rector*. Neither the police or food bank clients were impressed; they expected pastors to dress better than a T-shirt and sweatpants. Then Robert and Officer Chen, who provided off-duty security at the food bank, spotted each other. "Let him in," Officer Chen told his colleagues. "He runs this place."

The scene inside was chaos. Piles of clothing and twisted hangers covered the floor. The vestibule was stuffed with police and medics. Robert strained to see beyond them to his former living room. By squatting and duck-walking forward, he was able to see the checkout counter and the figure slumped behind the display case. Recognizing the figure's black curly hair and Hawaiian shirt, Robert fell to his knees and burst into tears. Two hands gripped his shoulders, and Terry said into his ear. "Our brother Dominic is gone."

Terry pulled Robert up and they hugged for a long time. As Robert gained some control, he heard wailing coming from the rectory kitchen.

"It's Mae," Terry said. "She found him."

Mae had lost the composure she'd summoned to report Nick's death. She was sitting beside the kitchen table, clutching her upper arms and rocking back and forth. A police officer sat next to her, making soothing noises. Lester and Spike stood in front of the sink in a protective stance.

The officer told Robert, "We've called her niece and the church deacon. They should be here any minute."

Robert knelt in front of Mae, took her hands, and enveloped them in his.

"Our brother Nick is gone," Mae moaned, "murdered in cold blood."

"What happened?" Robert asked. Mae, Terry, and the officer answered at the same time. He strained to comprehend.

"Nick ..."

"Dominic …"

"Mr. Monte …"

"… was counting behind …"

"… the till …"

"Today's take …"

"… when "someone …"

"A devil man …"

"… came in and shot …"

"… murdered …"

"Killed him."

Mae's voice prevailed. "I didn't hear nothing. I came back out of the kitchen and he was lying on the counter. The devil stayed awake last night planning this. And our take today besides the vouchers wasn't more than a hundred dollars. All that devil had to do was ask."

Terry said, "Friends, I doubt this was a robbery. It seems as though the devil decided to execute Nick."

Mae straightened up. "Why would he need to do that? Nick was no criminal and he wouldn't hurt a flea. And another thing … how did that devil get in here? I locked that front door; I turned the deadbolt latch myself and jiggled it to make sure, just like I always do." Behind her, Lester lifted his eyes to the ceiling and shook his head. A locked door was no obstacle in his former line of work.

"Why don't we wait until the detective gets here and can take your statements," the officer said. Just then Deacon Mary came into the kitchen, wearing a black shirt and clerical collar with a khaki skirt and loafers. The only unprofessional aspect to her appearance was the cowlick that stuck out from her white-blond pixie cut. She gave Robert a quick hug and then went over to Mae, who had begun moaning and rocking again. The police officer left the room. Terry went out to close the food bank.

Chapter Seven

～～

LESTER MOTIONED ROBERT OVER to the sink. Spike gave up his position and sat down next to Mae. In a hoarse voice meant to be a whisper, Lester said, "I've been standing here for these ten minutes thinking of a lot of things, and I think it would be better if I mentioned these things to you before the detective gets here."

Robert had been thinking too, along the lines of "Oh, dear God." Lester's vagabond days were not long behind him, and Robert had wondered more than once how involved the man still was with the crew under the freeway who were surviving on whatever they could beg, borrow, or steal.

"These things I've been thinking," Lester continued, "can generally be broken down into three main categories. And category one falls under the heading of 'building security.' And although I could discuss the security, or rather the lack of security, in every one of these grounds' buildings—including the church, the offices, the Sunday school rooms, social hall, and so on—for the sake of briefness, I'd better confine myself to this old rectory we're standing in."

"For the sake of briefness, you'd better speed up or the

detective will have come and gone before you're done," Robert said.

Lester sighed. "As I was saying, the security in this old rectory is pathetic at best. You see the bars on these kitchen windows? Everybody looks at them and thinks, Oh good, we're safe. But just the other day I had to fix some loose grout and all it took was a twist of my wrist to disengage the bar that was in the way. And all these other ground-floor windows. Where are the bars for them?"

Robert tried to interrupt, but Lester was too quick. "Now we'll proceed to that so-called deadbolt on the front door. That deadbolt would deter someone like me for about thirty seconds. And furthermore, do you know how many separate ingresses and egresses are in this old place? Not counting the front door and the side door, there are five—count 'em—*five*. The basement in and of itself has three, counting the hatch for the old coal chute."

"And your point is," said Robert, "that there are many ways besides and including the locked front door that someone could have got in to kill Nick. Point taken; on to the next point." He sighed and choked off a sob. "And damn it, Lester, I'm sorry to be so crabby but I've just lost a friend and parishioner. This is the second death we've had on these grounds in six months. After all we've done to reinvigorate this church and this neighborhood, Nick's murder will bring things to a screeching halt."

Lester patted Robert on the shoulder. "I counted Nick as my friend too. Which brings me to my second point. One of the reasons Nick and me got along so well was we recognized in each other what you could call kindred spirits. In another way of saying, Nick and me knew without ever talking about it that we'd both been on the other side of the law at one time or another, but that we'd both decided to get back on the right side. And both of us were helped along in that decision by the Good Lord giving us a push, and a lot more pushes after that."

Lester looked heavenward, as he always did when speaking of the Deity, and scratched his nose. "Like I said, we never talked in specific terms, but I guess I'm not entirely surprised that someone had it in for him. I just wish I knew who for sure. Which brings me to my third point."

Before he could continue, Mary interjected, "Robert, I'm going to walk Mae home. I talked to her niece on the phone and she'll meet us there. It's too upsetting for Mae to stay here with all the commotion and Nick lying dead in the next room. I'll talk to the police on the way out."

Robert gave her a sad salute and blew Mae a kiss. He motioned to Lester to join him at the table.

"Before you get to point three, I have something to add. I knew a little about Nick's past already. About four months ago, after he'd been coming to church for a while, he asked to talk to me confidentially. He wasn't making a formal confession, so I can tell the police about the conversation."

Lester's eyes widened. " 'Scuse me for interrupting," he interrupted, "but are you saying that if I was to go into one of those little rooms and unburden my soul, you couldn't tell anyone, not even the police?"

"That's right, and you wouldn't have to go into the little room to do it; confession can happen in my office, in the church, or even when we take Spike for a walk in the park. You may want to consider it."

Then Robert thought, *What am I doing telling all this to an ex-con who was in the building at the time of the murder?* He might as well press on. "Now, you said you wished you knew for sure. Does that mean you've got an idea who had it in for Nick? Is that your point three?"

Lester cast his eyes down. "Not that I'm willing and able to say at this time. My last point is that I'm caught up in a bind here and need to do some thinking on my own before I decide if I'll follow your lead and talk to the cops. I don't guess you can label what I just said as your kind of confession, can you?"

"You know the answer to that."

~~~

HE WASN'T GOING TO ditch the gun. No need to. No one could connect him with Dom.

Back in the day, Dominic had looked up to him like a dad, and that was fine. It suited his purposes. He'd needed a younger associate, and knew that young men wanted to be loyal, to feel a part of something important, to test their skills, to make somebody proud. Dom had the skills, that was for sure. He could charm the socks off anyone, make them feel like his best friend, work his way into their affairs, and then steal them blind.

That should have satisfied Dom—the chance to apprentice with the best. That and the money. That's the way he'd come up. The mistake he'd made with Dom was thinking they were alike in that way. Who knew that he had a conscience buried underneath, or that he'd found one after meeting up with those wackos at the church?

The whole experience had taught him a valuable lesson, so, at the time, he figured he owed it to Dom not to kill him, just as long as he left the area. But he hadn't. He'd moved to rival territory and set up shop as a do-gooder. Not even changing his name.

It was as if Dom was waving a red flag in his face, so he did what he should have done to begin with.

He'd had to kill Dom, after all.

Chapter Eight

～～～

BY 4:30 P.M. AN interview area had been set up in the parish hall next to the old rectory. The space was too big for the purpose, with its kitchen and stage, and a wood floor big enough to handle 200 dancing wedding guests.

Detective Joyce Hitchcock knew from her experience with the earlier death at Grace Church that this place wasn't set up like a precinct station. She could have used one of the Sunday school rooms upstairs to conduct the interviews, but the furniture was way too tiny for her six-foot-tall frame. And the room that would have been perfect was now an art gallery, with a bizarre metal sculpture sitting right in the middle on a big pedestal. It was labeled *Mother and Child*, and she was sure glad she wasn't the child—or the mother.

So, a corner of the parish hall it was.

"Officer Joyce!"

She fluffed out her shoulder-length blond hair and gave them all a big smile, which made her blue eyes sparkle. "Hey, Father Robert, Lester—and Daniel—and Deacon Mary. It's great to see you all again. I'm sorry as hell you have another murder on your hands."

Watch out Joyce, she told herself.

"But having said this," she continued, "I need to make it clear that I'm a detective now, and that I've been assigned to investigate this murder. And I hope you'll respect the fact that this is my first murder investigation, and that if I make one wrong step, such as showing preference to a witness or fraternizing with potential suspects, I'll be taken off this case so quick it'll make your head spin. I sure don't want my career jeopardized in that way, and I know that you don't either."

Daniel stepped forward and said, "Um, can I tell you one thing, and ask you one question, related to what you've just said?"

"Yes, Daniel, you can do that."

"Thank you," said the church organist. He wriggled his fingers, which appeared to be searching for a keyboard. "It's going to be hard for me, and probably for the others, to remember not to call you Officer Joyce anymore, not after you helped us capture the person who killed Ms. Clare this spring. So we hope you'll understand if we slip up and call you Officer Joyce once, or maybe twice, by mistake."

He looked at the others. "My question is, in order to call you by your right title, could you tell us again what your last name is?"

"It's Hitchcock. Detective Hitchcock. Here, I'll give you all my business card."

Father Robert came forward and shook her hand. "On behalf of Grace Parish, I welcome you back. We couldn't ask for a better officer, I mean detective, to lead this investigation. Whatever you need, we'll do our best to provide. And the staff here will fully cooperate by providing any information you request." He turned to the rest, looking particularly at Lester.

Deacon Mary stepped forward. "Detective Joyce, I mean Hitchcock, with your and Father Robert's permission, I'd like to arrange for a prayer vigil in the church's side chapel until Nick's funeral. Nick had lots of friends from the church, the thrift shop, and the food bank who'd like to pay their respects."

"Permission granted," said Detective Hitchcock.

Lester added, "And since some of those friends may not keep normal hours, I'll take my bedroll into that side chapel and provide security at nighttime."

Father Robert raised his eyebrows at Joyce; she raised hers back.

"Thanks for the offer, Lester, but I think you can lock up at ten," Robert said.

Detective Hitchcock added, "You're all free to go for now. Just keep yourselves available. All except for you, Lester. You stick around."

"Yes, ma'am," he said, coming forward.

"Lester, you and I need to have a serious talk. I'm going to interview Ms. Perkins first, and you second. And I hope for your sake I won't need to do a follow-up."

"Yes, ma'am," Lester answered. "I guess since I was under suspicion for Ms. Clare's murder, I'll be suspected for this one too. It's the least you have to do."

Chapter Nine

~~~

TUESDAY MORNING, FATHER ROBERT called Daniel, Deacon Mary and Mrs. Evans into his office to begin planning Nick's funeral. Mae Perkins also insisted on being there, even though she was groggy from the sleeping pills her doctor had prescribed. The police were still trying to locate Nick's next of kin, so the date and time of the service were up in the air. Robert started by asking each one to say a prayer of thanks for Nick's life, mentioning something special about him.

Daniel appreciated his deep knowledge of music. Mrs. Evans gave him credit for being a hard worker and good salesman at the thrift shop. Deacon Mary admitted that she'd been drawn to his good looks and muscular build, adding that he was always willing to serve the down-and-out types she brought to the thrift store, even if they didn't have a voucher.

"At least we know what hymn he wanted," said Mae, after proclaiming Nick to be her best friend and a true disciple of Christ. " 'His Eye is on the Sparrow.' He told Daniel and me yesterday, as if he knew it was his only chance."

"I'm sorry, Mae, I'm not familiar with that hymn, and I'm sure it's not in our hymnal," said Mrs. Evans.

"Then why did my mama and I sing it at every funeral at this very church when I was a girl?" Mae said. "Granted, that was way before your time."

"Um, actually you're both correct," said Daniel. "Even though the song isn't in our blue 1982 hymnal, Mrs. Evans, it has a long tradition as a church hymn, and has always been in the hymnal of the African Methodist Episcopal Church. And now 'His Eye is on the Sparrow' is in one of our newer hymnals, called *Lift Every Voice and Sing*. Since we own copies of that hymnal, we can legally reproduce it in the funeral bulletin, as long as we include the publishing credit."

Mae smiled, leaned her head against the chair, and dozed.

"Sorry I'm late." Stacy Chase unwound her paisley shawl while looking for a chair.

"Hi, Stacy," said Robert. "We're reminiscing about Nick and beginning to plan his funeral."

"Oh. I thought you were planning the reception." Seeing their somber faces, she began twisting the shawl ends. "I guess I've put the cart before the horse."

"Hello, Ms. Stacy, we're glad you're here," said Daniel, offering her his chair. "Could you give your prayer of thanks for Mr. Nick and say what was special about him for you?"

Why don't I just let Daniel be the pastor around here? thought Robert.

"Sorry, Daniel," Stacy said, "I'm not one for praying out loud. It's horrible that Nick was murdered and just one hour after I was in the shop. I had heart palpitations all night. Rick didn't want me to come here today; he thinks one of the street people did it and might go after anyone they think is a witness."

She paused. "And so I didn't tell him. Anyway, I liked Nick, even though he was the worst dresser I've ever seen. But he knew a lot about antiques and collectibles. And he made me laugh." Tears were rolling down her face. "I loved it when he wriggled his eyebrows."

Robert handed her a tissue. "That was a beautiful tribute,

Stacy. And you brought up an important point. Your husband isn't the only one who will be inclined to stay away from the church, especially since this is the second death on these grounds, and a particularly brutal one. I'll be talking to the vestry about it later today."

Mae raised her head. "There's no need to worry about retribution. Nick came to me last night in a dream and said not to worry about that, that he was up there now watching over us."

Robert pulled two tissues from the box and balled them up before beginning his tribute. "I'm grateful that Nick came into my life. Nick was special, we all know that. People like him don't usually come to church and we need more of them. He made me laugh, and trusted me with some heavy confidences.

"Somewhere along the way, he'd found his better self. He taught me not to worry and fuss so much. And this may sound strange, but when I was with him and Terry from the food bank I felt like one of the guys. I've been a loner most of my life, but those two dragged me out of my shell. We went to all the Sounders soccer matches, movies, fishing …. I guess it's time to stop; I've run out of Kleenex."

Chapter Ten

~~~

D ETECTIVE HITCHCOCK LOOKED UP from her laptop at the man standing in front of the interview table.

"Sit down Lester, you're in luck. You won't have to tell on Mr. Jones, the one who got into a beef with the deceased a few weeks ago at the thrift shop. Luckily, Ms. Perkins was present when it happened and heard the warning you gave the deceased yesterday. Now, were there any witnesses to your conversation with Mr. Jones yesterday on the street corner?"

Lester squirmed in his seat. "I sure wish you could violate your procedures and reference Nick as Nick and Mae as Mae. That word 'deceased' sends shivers up my spine, and calling that lowlife by his last name, which I didn't even know, but which is the same as mine, makes me want to gag."

Joyce started to answer, "I … agggh!" A crashing piano chord had interrupted them. "What's your organist doing in here playing the piano? We posted signs telling everyone to stay out of this room."

"Nah," answered Lester, "it's Joe White. He lives in the public housing tower across the street and tends to ignore signs. He used to accompany the community chorus before he lost his memory. We let him come in to play; it tones up the place."

"I guess it's okay, since he's lost his memory," said Joyce. "It'll provide sound cover for my interviews."

Lester continued, "As I was going to say next, ma'am, I knew this very day would come, sooner or later, ever since I left the streets this summer and moved into the attic of the rectory next door. As a bit of background, you may or may not realize that street people don't hate their brethren that move up in life, not as long as those brethren remember where they came from."

Joyce waved her hand in a gesture of impatience.

But Lester would not be rushed. "That's why I include the nearby street corners on my daily security rounds. I've been able to step in between a few conflicts and defuse them, which I figure not only helps church security, but allows the police to attend to more serious matters."

He waited for her compliment, which was not forthcoming, so he went on, "But despite what you say, about me being off the hook, now's the very time I have to answer that question from the old labor song my daddy taught me. And can you guess what that question is?"

"No I can't," said the detective with a sigh. "So why don't you tell me."

" 'Which Side Are You On,' "Lester answered. "I don't think I need to repeat all of the words for you, because the song is so famous. Now the sides they were on in this song were the union and the bosses. But I've exter-apolated from that and decided that my side in this case is the downtrodden, which I used to be, versus those that trod on the downtrodden. And that includes the lowlifes that snitch off their fellow downtrodden."

Joyce shook her head. "You've extrapolated? Congratulations. I've never even tried to do that."

Lester raised his arms over his head, fingers intertwined, brought them to his chest, and cracked his knuckles. "But in this case I'm choosing to view this guy Al as someone who's up to no good, not for neither side. So now I'll begin."

"Thank you," said Joyce, shaking her head slightly.

"Al showed up a few months ago," Lester began. "Said he was from Spokane and looking for less nasty weather. He has a funny way of talking that I can't put a finger on, except that it has something to do with how he pronounces his a's and e's and i's and o's and u's."

"His vowels," summarized Joyce.

"He's only been at that freeway entrance an hour or two at a time and only one or two days a week. Almost like he was—"

"A lookout," they both said.

Lester patted his shirt pocket. "I'd swear he has another source of income. He's always got cigarettes, which he refuses to share, and I sure wish I had one now. Except that I'm trying to quit. It's too much hassle walking down the three flights of those rectory stairs and out the front door to light up."

"You're doing great, Lester," Joyce said. "Just a few more questions. "How did the de—ah—Nick act yesterday when you told him what Al said?"

Lester took a moment to answer. "I'm straining my brain trying to put it into words, because there was more than one thing going on at once. The first thing was, Nick just about jumped out of his skin when I told him. It was like I was talking about someone he never expected to see again. But then when Mae reminded him about the incident at the shop, he seemed—what's the word—relieved?"

"That works," said Joyce.

"You should ask Ms. Perkins if she thought so too. Say, how did you find out Al's last name?"

"You weren't the only one who didn't trust him," said Joyce. We brought him in a few weeks ago for suspicion of theft and ran his prints. We're trying to locate him now." She paused. "Shit, what am I doing telling you all this?"

"Don't worry, ma'am, I can keep a confidence, and I'll disregard the swearing. Al probably took off the minute he saw those police cars coming up the hill to the old rectory. Unless he—"

Joyce interrupted, "Where were you when Nick was shot, which was, as near as we can tell at three twenty?"

"I was up in my room eating a sandwich that I'd made in the kitchen. I saved the leftovers for you as proof. And also, when I heard all the commotion Mae made when she went upstairs, I came down to the first floor. Terry was already right there next to Nick. The police came a few minutes after that."

Joyce continued, "Who else was in the building?"

"Let's see, besides Mae and Terry, I saw Arlis the food bank bookkeeper, but that don't mean anything. There's so many entrances and exits—"

"We know, Lester. Later on, we'll map out every single ingress and egress to the old rectory and the food bank. I sure wish Raymond was here to do that part. I'm hopeless at three-dimensional stuff. I asked the lieutenant to assign him. I reminded him about Raymond's part in wrapping up the earlier murder, but it probably won't happen."

"You mean Officer Chen?" Lester asked. "He's a good guy. Short as he is, when he works off-duty security at the food bank, it runs like clockwork, and he's backed me up when I need it around the church."

The front door to the parish hall slammed. Joyce looked up. "Ray!"

"Joyce!" he answered.

When Officer Chen reached the interview table, she stood, reached down, and clapped him on the shoulder.

"Thanks for requesting me," he told her. "I was getting tired of foot patrol in the International District."

Joyce, who remained standing, towered over both men. "Let's go tour the rectory."

"The interior door to the parish hall opened and Henry, the sexton, walked in.

"I'm locking up. Out you go," he announced.

Lester walked over to him. "Hey, Henry, just the guy we need. You know every inch of these grounds and these officers here need all the information they can get on the old rectory, so they can solve Nick's murder."

Henry started to speak, but Lester talked over him. "Now I know you need to get your lunch break, but since this is police business, I bet they'll spring for a meal at Mario's on Madison Street afterward, won't you, officers?"

The desperate look on Lester's face prompted Joyce to say, "Sure. But Lester, you come too. That's an order."

Lester smiled and tipped the green Sounders cap that Nick had given him, with its blue Space Needle logo.

AFTER TOURING THE OLD rectory and listening to Henry reminisce over thirty years of building maintenance issues, Joyce and Raymond took an extra-long lunch at a nearby Sushi place.

"Ray, I know you've spent lots of time around the rectory and thrift shop on your security gig. Did you see anything new on the tour? I figure the bad guy probably hid somewhere until the shop closed at three."

Officer Chen nodded. "I knew about the two entrances on the first floor and the basement door down the slope below. I hadn't noticed the old coal chute before. Actually the staff has been good about installing decent locks and maintaining key control, considering that there's really no one person in charge of the building."

He pulled out his tablet computer. "So I'll need to interview Ms. Evans the store manager, Terry from the food bank, Pastor Robert, and the day and night sextons and hope that—"

"FYI," Joyce said, "it's Father Robert, not Pastor Robert."

Officer Chen made a note. "What I did notice was how many nooks and crannies the place has. The basement has so many stacks of furniture and boxes that twenty-five people could have hidden there. Also, upstairs I counted ..." he checked his screen, "ten interior doors that aren't locked. The best place for the bad guy to hide would have been behind the door from the kitchen to the basement. Assuming that the three main doors were locked, he could have hid there until the shop closed, and he knew Nick was by himself. He would have heard Ms. Perkins going through the kitchen to the bathroom, leaving him clear to come into the shop and do the deed."

"That makes sense," Joyce said. "Unless he was one of the key holders, or had managed to get ahold of one. Then he could have come through the front door after Ms. Perkins locked it. So at this point, it could have been an inside or outside job."

Joyce stood up. "God, we've got to go, and we still haven't begun to discuss a possible motive or who the hell was this Nick that he needed executing. I want you there when I interview Father Robert and Terry Buffett. After that, get going on the key research and talking to the folks who live around here. That's another thing that's going to drive us nuts. We've got the rich retirees in their condo tower across the street, everyone else who lives in the public housing tower, plus the felons at the halfway house. What a mess!"

Chapter Eleven

~~~

Detective Joyce had granted Terry and Robert's request to be interviewed together, after meeting with them separately to nail down their whereabouts at the time of the murder.

She began by saying, "You both seem to be in the clear. Father, two neighbors saw you running down the stairs and out the side door of your condo complex right after Mr. Monte was murdered. And Terry, you and your bookkeeper—uh, Arlis—verify that you were meeting in her office. So, I'm wondering, why do you want a team interview? I know you're friends, but still, this is outside of normal procedure."

Robert and Terry looked at each other. "Age before beauty," Terry said.

"Okay, pal. Detective … would you let me call you Detective Joyce? I promise to use your last name in public."

"Whatever makes you the most comfortable," she said.

"Thanks. So, Terry and I got to know Nick as well as anyone over the past six months or so. That's when he started attending church. Two weeks later he was volunteering at Terry's food bank. When the thrift shop opened in August, he volunteered there too. He joined the men's Bible study. In other words, he got involved."

"He was a great guy," Terry added. "Sorry, Robert, but he wasn't the sort of guy who usually hangs out at church. He was funny, irreverent, didn't stand on ceremony, and knew more ways to cuss people out than you can imagine. The two of us hit it off right away; it helped that we both loved soccer. Before long we were hanging out at least once a week. Then Nick corralled Robert into joining us."

Robert took over. "I was never one for sports. But here's what was special about Nick: after we'd talked a few times, minister to parishioner, he saw that my social life was just about non-existent. I've found a wonderful romantic partner in Molly, but we've had to be careful not to—"

Detective Joyce clapped her hands. "You and Molly? The woman in red? That is so cool. I guess there's hope for me yet."

Officer Chen stopped note taking on his tablet and looked up. "I assume I won't be recording this part of the interview?"

Joyce ducked her head. "Okay, back to business. So what did you two learn about the de … Nick's background?"

"Let me start by saying that he never made a formal confession, so I'm free to tell you what I know," said Robert. "I've made some notes."

"Robert, polish your lenses first, or we'll be here all night," said Terry. "Remember what happened last Sunday when you tried to read your sermon?"

Robert's lenses were so thick that they bumped into his eyelashes, which kept the lenses perpetually cloudy.

He took them off, found a cloth in his pocket, and polished them. Putting them back on, he said, "Okay, all set. Let's see. At our first meeting, Nick told me that he'd moved here recently from Canada—Vancouver, B.C., to be exact. He was a U.S. citizen, but said he'd been in Canada since he was in his late teens. I'm not sure if he was orphaned or abandoned by his family, but in any case, he fell in with a crew of thieves.

"His situation reminded me of Oliver Twist because he said there was an older man, a kind of Fagin, who ran the operation. I got the impression that Nick was his favorite, or protégé. Nick didn't go into detail, but the gist was he was trained to use his natural charm to gain the trust of whomever the boss was targeting.

"The targets weren't little old ladies; they were business owners. Nick would use what the target told him to set up thefts of merchandise, cargo loads of merchandise that the ring his boss ran would arrange to send overseas for a big profit."

Joyce asked, "Did this ring, or the ringmaster, have a name?"

"Not that he told me," answered Robert, looking at Terry.

"This is the first I've heard any of this, except that he'd come down from Canada. I thought of Nick as a smart guy who'd bounced around a lot. And that didn't bother me, because that's been my life, too. And here he was, settling down in one place to do good work, just like I did."

"Did he mention any Asian connection?" asked Officer Chen. "At a joint training last year, I heard lots of talk about goods being smuggled to Asia from Canada."

Robert shook his head. "What he seemed to want to talk about was the reason he came back to the States. One of the business people he'd been told to target had an aunt who died. The guy was going to be out of town on the day of the funeral and was upset that no one would be there. So Nick offered to go to represent the family."

Joyce held up her hand. "Does this have something to do with any criminal activity?"

"I don't care if it does," Robert answered. "I want to give you an accurate picture of the man Nick became."

She waved him on.

"So he went to the funeral, which was held at Holy Trinity Anglican church in East Vancouver. Anglican is the same as Episcopalian, or near enough. You probably know that East Vancouver isn't the tourist part of town. It's poor, dirty, and industrial, with lots of transients and addicts. Holy Trinity is one of the oldest churches in the city, just like Grace church here in Seattle."

Before Robert could continue, the sound of a heavy-duty floor machine propelled them all a few inches off their seats.

"Henry, Henry!" Robert yelled, standing up and walking toward the monster. "I told you not to disturb us in here. Henry!"

The machine went silent.

Henry the sexton's favorite activity was keeping the floors shiny, and he'd begged and begged until the vestry authorized the purchase of the top floor polisher on the market. He used it as often as he could, much like a suburban homeowner spending every Saturday on their oversized riding lawn mower. And as a certified geezer, he appreciated being able to lean against the handle as he polished.

Robert ended their heated exchange, shouting, "Five minutes!"

He returned to the group and said, "It's not worth it. Let's go to the sanctuary. He polished that yesterday."

Joyce and Raymond looked at each other. They knew that procedure called for a standard-sized, bland interview room furnished with a scarred table and as many uncomfortable chairs as needed. But Joyce also knew that their current interviewees might well be more forthcoming in spiritual-type surroundings.

"Let's go," she said.

Chapter Twelve

~~~

ONCE SETTLED IN THE sanctuary on the formerly red, now faded pink cushions atop the dark-veined fir pews, Robert took up his narrative.

"Nick walked into the church expecting to be the only mourner, but found twenty people there. There were candles on the altar, a minister in full vestments, and an organist. That was when he was converted—when he found out after the service that the other mourners hadn't known the relative, but had buried her anyway as one their own. The minister explained that it was a service that the church provided for any of the city's dead whose bodies were unclaimed.

"Nick realized that his target hadn't even paid the pittance required for a proper burial and was willing to let the church pick up the tab. He also realized that the church would do the same for him, and for anyone else who needed it.

"After that day, he began to extricate himself from the criminal ring. He told his employer that he had some family business to take care of and left B.C. for the States. He was headed to California, but happened on Grace Church when he stopped in Seattle. It reminded him of Holy Trinity, and he decided to stick around for a service and to talk to me. Then he stayed on for a while, even though he must have been worried about being so close to the border."

"Did he seem to have a lot of money to spend?" asked Officer Chen.

"Not that I could see." Robert hesitated. "But now I wonder. One Sunday the ushers came up after the service saying that there were a thousand dollars in large bills in the collection plate. The same thing happened at least three more times. I can't remember the exact amount, but it was enough to make up our budget shortfall for this year."

Terry said, "You know, our cash donations at the food bank have gone up, too."

"Interesting," said Joyce. "Anything else you can tell us?"

They had nothing of substance to add, and the interview ended. Joyce asked them to find out what they could from people at the parish and food bank.

Then she asked, "Mind if Raymond and I stay here in the church a while longer?"

"Just make sure the door locks behind you." Robert said.

"Seems too bad you have to do that," said Raymond. "Not to be preachy, but the Buddhist shrines in Seattle are open all the time."

"They're lucky to have people available to welcome visitors," said Robert. "It's the same way in the European countries. A retired priest hangs out during the day, keeping an eye on things and gossiping with the neighborhood ladies who drop in. Maybe I'll take on that job when I'm too old to climb the altar steps."

Robert and Terry walked from the church into the courtyard that contained the memorial garden. Once the heavy door shut, Terry said, "Something came to me in there, but I didn't want to bring it up before talking to you. A few months ago we had some missing inventory at our warehouse in South

Seattle. Whole pallets full of canned goods, paper goods and dry goods."

"You have a warehouse?" asked Robert. "I thought all the donations were stored here at the food bank."

"That was true ten years ago when we started, but we've been in growth mode. You see how many people we serve. Where do you think all that food comes from? These food barrels set up around the church? You obviously haven't been paying attention at our annual meetings. We're a million dollar a year business." Terry swooped low to pick up a discarded paper bag that had held a food bank lunch. "You think this location has a lot of clients? We also supply satellite operations all over Western Washington."

"Okay, okay. I'm impressed; I really am. So Terry, what's with the missing inventory?"

"Three years ago one of our corporate donors offered us space in his warehouse for free. And by the way, our last fund drive netted enough to add refrigeration to that warehouse this year." Terry stopped his testimonial at a look from Robert.

"Anyway, about four months ago, we noticed we were running out of product when we weren't before. The smaller food banks started hollering because their orders weren't being filled. Until then, our inventory control was nonexistent. We were too busy feeding people, and I guess we figured, how low do you have to go before you'd rip off a food bank?

"Now we finally have a decent system in place, so we can track what's coming in and going out and where it's going and if it arrives and if the same amount arrives that went out."

Robert gave a thumbs up. "That's the best description of inventory control I've heard." He clapped Terry on the back for emphasis.

"Thanks, bro. So when you told the detective about Nick's background, a light went on. I really don't want to believe he was conning me. I really don't. But here we have Nick himself telling you how good he was at conning businesses out of their stuff. And remember how little time it took him to become our new best friend."

"Let's say he was ripping you off," said Robert, "which I don't believe, by the way. Assuming he had partners in the deal, why would they want to murder him? And even if he turned and was ripping them off, it's hard to see how a few thousand dollars would get you a shot in the head."

"I do think we need to tell Detective Joyce, but let's take a day first to do some investigating ourselves. She told us to ask around."

"Okay," said Terry. "I'll ask our warehouse owner if he's had missing inventory. Robert paused. can't believe I didn't do that right away. Running a business was not part of my life plan when I offered to give away food ten years ago. I'll pass around Nick's description, too, and I guess I'll have to update my board of directors.

"And speaking of them," he added, "Shit, I could just slap myself for recruiting those Chamber of Commerce types."

Robert checked his watch. "Speaking of boards in general," he said, "I've got a meeting with mine right now. But first, I'm going to take a walk around the block to psych myself up. I'm sure glad Bishop Adams is behind me for this catastrophe."

He looked straight up into the sky. "Nick, this is for you, and you'd better figure out a way to buy us a round of beers when we find out who killed you."

Chapter Thirteen

"What do we know, Ray?"

"Just a sec while I do some formatting," he said.

Joyce took advantage of the break to look up at the stained glass and farther up to the dark-fir ceiling that was shaped like the prow of a ship. Her neck cracked. "Boy that feels good!"

Raymond answered, "Dominic Paul Monte, white Caucasian male age forty-five, six feet one inch tall, two hundred thirty pounds. Born to Mary Kelly, a nurse, in St. Paul, Minnesota. Father unknown, although she must have produced a surname.

"Attended Catholic schools until eighth grade. Attended Central High School for three years. Played football and on the swim team. Grades ranged from A to F depending upon the subject. Arrested twice for speeding and underage drinking.

"Left home at age seventeen. Kept in contact with his mother until she died of cancer in 2000. No other known relatives.

"Turned up in Vancouver, B.C., in the 1980s. Employed by Skyline Importers. Started out in the warehouse driving forklift. Worked his way into sales."

"Stop!" said Joyce. "How did you find all this out? We've been stuck indoors interviewing all day."

"I was up half the night and did some Googling and texting during the interviews—especially after the Father mentioned what he knew about Mr. Monte's background. I've got a girlfriend in the criminal records department who should be working for the NSA."

"A girlfriend?"

"Forget it, Joyce. She's not *that* kind of girlfriend. It's just a term. Now, if you're ready, I've got more."

He hurried on, "Mr. Monte left that company and seemed to become more of a freelancer. He may not have been a criminal when he started at Skyline, but he was when he left. The Mounties ran around in circles trying to bust him, but never got anywhere. Mr. Nick had some big time protection.

"There are three major theft rings operating up there, but he stayed close to the one run by a guy named Joe Spano. I guess I should say 'allegedly' run. The guy's so well-hidden, the only picture they have on file is from his high school graduation."

Raymond looked up. "I'm just speculating now. Mr. Monte may or may not have been involved in larcenous activities down here. He didn't arrive all that long ago, so he wouldn't have had much time to take up his former line of work, and the volunteering he did for the church and the food bank doesn't fit that life. Especially if he was the source of the cash donations."

Joyce cracked her neck again and then rolled her head down and around her shoulders.

"Watch out," Raymond said, "you could paralyze yourself."

"Thanks for the concern. Okay, Mr. Nick is a criminal who may or may not have gone straight. So now let's talk suspects."

"I think we have to go on the assumption that someone from his past caught up to him. We could fiddle around and arrest Lester to make the brass happy, but why waste time? The only real suspect is Al Jones, the guy by the freeway. He may have been sent down to find Nick and bide his time until the coast was clear."

"*A e i o u*," Joyce said.

"And sometimes *y*. So what?"

"Lester told me that Mr. Jones pronounced his verbs funny. Sounds Canadian to me."

"Genius, Joyce."

"But why decide to execute Mr. Monte in a thrift shop with lines of people outside and at least three in the building? Something else is going on here, or I hope it is, because I don't want my first big case to be open and shut. We could build our reputations on this one, Ray."

"Genius again, boss."

"Okay, let's get out of here and split up. You find out more about who was in and out of the old rectory and I'll go brief the lieutenant. I am *so* glad he gets to deal with the press and not me."

"I wouldn't be so sure," said Raymond. "If they get too nasty, he may use you as a shield."

"Thanks for that, and I'll see you back here at 0800 tomorrow. Or rather, back in the parish hall. You bring the coffee. Make mine a double Americano."

"Sorry, sir. I only drink green tea and I make it at home."

"Not tomorrow you don't."

"Yes, sir, Detective Hitchcock, sir." He gave a crisp salute and departed, saying, "Be sure the door locks behind you."

Raymond took the exterior church stairs three at a time and gave a hop at the bottom. He didn't know where this thing with Joyce was going, but she was sure a good sparring partner.

Chapter Fourteen

~~~

RAYMOND'S NEXT STOP WAS the old rectory, floor two, to interview Mrs. Evans, the thrift store manager. He hoped she was a busybody.

Mrs. Evans ushered him in, removing a pile of flashing Christmas lights from the chair. "I'm sorry for the clutter, Officer, but I have to test another fifty or so strings before the holiday season. You can never tell with donations."

The office was packed with more little things than his granny's apartment, but all of it was dusted and arranged by height on rows of shelving.

"Officer, I was expecting the detective to interview me."

How should he reply? Snarky, obsequious, sincere? He felt like snarky but decided on sincere, with a dash of flattery.

"I apologize, Mrs. Evans. She's been called to headquarters for a press conference. Otherwise, she certainly would have taken the interview.

"Mrs. Evans, you've already reported that you were in the building from eight thirty a.m. to two thirty p.m. yesterday. I understand you came up to your office and didn't return downstairs until just before leaving. But as the person who

oversaw the transition of this building from a rectory into
a multi-service agency, you must be its eyes and ears, so to
speak."

He paused. "For instance, you probably recognize many
of the voices you hear from this office. We know that Terry
Buffett, Arlis Bell, and Lester Jones were in and out, and we'd
like you to write down the approximate times you heard them.
Is there anyone else you can identify?"

Mrs. Evans looked at him over the top of her rectangular
scarlet-colored glasses. "Shouldn't you be asking Terry and
Arlis? Other than my cubbyhole, the second floor is their space.
And you must ask Father Vickers about Lester's whereabouts.
I've made it clear to Father that I take no responsibility for
monitoring our new night sexton. I assume you know that Mr.
Jones was very recently a street person and was arrested earlier
this year on a criminal matter."

"And never charged," Raymond said. "Yes, I know. Now, I'm
asking you what you observed and heard yesterday." Raymond
took out a traditional notepad from his back pocket and poised
his pencil, certain that this move would be more effective than
entering data into his tablet.

She brought out her own notebook and a sharper pencil.
"I've made some notes." She showed him as she read aloud:

> 8:35: Arrived, and toured the shop before it opened to
> make sure everything was in its place.
> 9:05: Came upstairs to my office.

She continued through the morning in great detail, covering
not only the second floor, but also the first, recognizing the
voices of Dr. Lucy, Daniel, Stacy, and a few of the thrift shop's
frequent customers. She also nailed the arrival and departure
times of the person who made the weekly bottled water delivery,
which she felt was a waste of the church's scarce resources.

When she was describing activity on the second floor at

10:30 a.m., Raymond interrupted. "Wait a minute; you say a board member of the food bank arrived on this floor with Terry?"

Her mouth twitched. "Surely Terry told you when you interviewed him?"

No he didn't, Raymond thought, *because after I cleared him for the time of the murder I forgot to ask, and he forgot to mention it because he was in shock.*

"Of course. We just like to independently verify when we can. So you'll understand if I ask you the name of the board member."

"I'm surprised that you think I'd have that information, but as it happens, I keep a copy of the food bank's newsletter for reference." She pulled it out of a blue folder.

"Ed Grafton, who's new to the board. He owns a trucking company with offices here and in Portland. That will be a big help because he's promised to haul supplies to the satellite food banks when his trucks are available.

"Sheila Foster, a principal in Wiggins, Foster and Schnabel, is the board president, and I must say, Terry's lucky to have her. Professionalism hasn't been a strong suit at the food bank, but she's getting things on a sound footing."

Her mouth twitched again. "Her only failure has been enforcing a dress code for Terry.

"I'm sure Arlis can provide you with Mr. Grafton's contact information. I see that Terry is out, as he usually is. Here are their pictures."

"Mrs. Evans, I am impressed." *You just saved me about an hour.* "I wish all witnesses had the facts at their fingertips like you do. Please keep your eyes and ears open, and call me if you learn anything more. Here's my card."

Mrs. Evans patted her hair before taking the card and inserting it into the Plexiglas holder on her desk. She then nodded him out the door.

Chapter Fifteen

~~~

AFTER HIS MEETING WITH Mrs. Evans, Raymond Chen stopped by the food bank office to get contact information on the new board member Ed Grafton and the board president. Arlis Bell had definitely been in shock yesterday, and if anything she looked worse today. She sat next to the north-facing window, bundled in a heavy sweater. Her feet were inches away from a space heater. He knew she was a blonde, but today her hair and skin seemed the same color as her sweater: light gray. They knew each other slightly, because she cut the check for his off-duty security work. He decided to be honest with her.

"Arlis, you look terrible. Were you a friend of the ... I mean Nick?"

She didn't turn from the window. "He pretended that I was an heiress who was slumming by working at the food bank. He'd say things like, "Arlis, I'm surprised you're here so early after the symphony benefit last night. He'd check out events in the paper and pretend that I'd been there. He'd even pretend that my picture was in one of the local magazines and go on about my gown and my hairstyle. He'd say things like 'That pageboy really set off your diamond earrings.' "

After a minute, Arlis continued, "No, he wasn't a close friend; I know that. But no one's ever paid attention to me like he did. And I doubt that anyone ever will again. That's why I'm taking this so badly."

Raymond wanted to reassure her, but couldn't think of anything that would help, so he said, "I only met him a couple of times, when he called for security at the thrift shop. So I didn't see that side of him. Anyway, I don't want to intrude; I just need the contact information for the board member who was here yesterday, and also the board president."

She kicked the heater and turned toward him. "You mean Mr. Thug and Ms. Snotty? Sure. I hope you rake them over the coals."

Raymond's fingers faltered on his tablet and he accidentally pressed the music app. An electronic dance beat filled the room.

"Sorry," he said, when he'd finally managed to silence it. "Mr. Thug? Do you have any evidence to back that up?"

"Just talk to him for thirty seconds and you'll see what I mean. No, I don't have evidence, just my so-called women's intuition."

"Okay. Thanks, Arlis. We could use some intuition in this case, so don't turn it off."

As he was turning to go, he stopped and said, "I wouldn't have compared you to a socialite. I think of you more as a writer, like Emily Dickinson, or someone current, like Amy Tan."

"How'd you guess, Raymond? How'd you guess? *Au revoir.*"

The food bank line was still backed up around the corner. Raymond wondered if it ever went away. Then he noticed a familiar figure.

"Ms. Perkins, is that you?" Mae was standing in the line wearing a knit cap and a torn jacket that looked like it came from the thrift store free box.

"Shhhh," she hissed.

"Come over here," he hissed back. "That's an order, ma'am."

"Save my place," she told the man in front of her, and edged herself over to Raymond.

"Now why'd you go and blow my cover? And don't tell me I don't fit into this food bank line. Many's the time I've stood in this very line at the end of the month before my check came. You'd be surprised who you find here. Schoolteachers, college students. The saddest are the mothers needing formula for their babies."

"I know, ma'am. My granny uses the food bank too, the one in the International District. Now, what is it you hope to find out by going undercover?"

"I'm trying to find someone who saw that devil come in or leave the shop yesterday." She looked up and down the street as she spoke. "My luck will be better tomorrow. That's when the ones who were here yesterday will be back. And just so you don't have another conniption, Lester is down by the freeway asking about that man who threatened Nick."

"Thanks for telling me. I guess I can't stop you from standing in the line, but if you find out anything, or don't feel safe, let me know. Keep your phone on you."

Mae laughed until tears rolled down her cheeks. "Cell? You think I have a cell? No thanks, I'll scream if I'm in trouble and call you from a real phone. Now, go on out there and help me find that devil. Nick's counting on us."

Chapter Sixteen

~~~

MOLLY FERGUSON WAS TEMPORARILY working at the Grace Church office instead of the Bishop's office. Last evening, when she'd located Bishop Adams and told him about the murder, he'd asked her to help out at Grace Church, and as he put it, "monitor the scene."

The circumstances were tragic; she'd met Nick and found him to be delightful and a good friend to Robert. Despite all this, she couldn't help but smile at the goings-on around her. There were three women in the church's tiny office, none of them sitting at the secretary's desk. She was standing at the counter window helping walk-in visitors with a variety of needs: bus passes, referrals, sympathy. Behind her, Mrs. Evans had the phone to her ear, telling a caller from the press that there would be no further statement from the church on the tragic incident yesterday and how it might or might not be connected with the incident last spring, and that no, the funeral had not been scheduled yet.

Stacy Chase had deposited her laptop next to the copy machine on the counter and was soliciting volunteers to help with the funeral and reception. Ordinarily Arlis, Grace

Church's part-time secretary, would be sitting at the desk, but she was too upset to be around people.

Molly knew that Arlis had had a huge crush on Nick, so it was no wonder she was mourning. As a matter of fact, she'd been concerned that Nick might take advantage of Arlis and had asked Terry to intervene. Terry reported back that Nick was bewildered, saying that he only wanted to cheer up Arlis— that it made him feel good to make other people feel good. He wasn't interested in seducing and abandoning anyone at this stage in his life. Molly had been puzzled at this; Nick was far from a decrepit, over-the-hill single man. Why wouldn't he want to court an intelligent, like-minded single woman?

Then she thought about a book she'd read, titled *Dakota*. The writer, Kathleen Norris, had attended retreats at a Roman Catholic monastery in the Midwest. Norris observed how the monks treated their women retreatants—the rich, poor, the homely and beautiful—with exactly the same interest and courtesy.

Was it possible that Nick had been an undercover monk?

Even at her most cheerful, Arlis would not be your first choice to meet and greet the public and answer the phone. Her strong suit was accounting and computer technology. That was why there were three women here to replace her today. Molly knew that Mrs. Evans and Stacy both felt entitled to run the show, and regarded the bishop's secretary as an interloper, even though she was now a member of Grace Parish. But today there was a temporary truce.

There were no supplicants at the window now, and Molly thought back to yesterday, when she'd been enjoying a quiet afternoon at her desk in Diocesan House, the bishop's office. Bishop Anthony Adams was away on a visit to St. Clements Church in Longview, a logging town along the Columbia River one hundred miles south of Seattle. As she put address labels on the thousand old-fashioned newsletters the Bishop insisted on sending out to his flock, Molly had listened to old-school jazz on the radio and reminisced about the good times she'd enjoyed with her late husband Jim.

When she'd met him in 1968, Jim Ferguson had been twenty years older, and had shepherded her out of Beatlemania into the cool jazz scene, which he'd entered in the 1950s. One of its famous habitués had been Mose Allison, whose world-weary voice was at this moment telling her, "I'm the one they call the seventh son."

Along the way, she replaced her psychedelic outfits with stylish dresses, suits, and pants. Jim whistled extra loud when she wore red, so she decided to make it her signature color. Today she was wearing a red shrug sweater over a red and black patterned T-shirt, set off by the kind of black jeans that looked like slacks.

Here she was, about to become engaged to a man much nearer her age, two years younger, in fact. Where Jim had been tall, handsome, and socially prominent, Robert was shorter—though still attractive—and socially out of it. Both her men were intelligent conversationalists, and both loved to hug. She felt just as content, just as safe, just as able to follow her own pursuits, and just as in love with Robert. And since he wasn't musically inclined, he wouldn't try to influence her musical taste and therefore wouldn't object when she listened to jazz. She was a very lucky woman.

As she was folding and stamping the last of the z's, the 3:30 news had come on. That's how she'd learned that the old rectory at Grace Church was the scene of a murder. She'd texted Robert to find out if he was safe, tracked down the bishop, canceled her evening book group, and ten minutes later had locked up the office and was on her way to Robert's condo to wait for him.

Chapter Seventeen

TUESDAY MORNING, DETECTIVE JOYCE looked up at the fir-beamed ceiling of the Grace Church Parish Hall, her temporary office. She couldn't seem to get enough of ceilings lately. It was probably because the church's ceilings were worth looking at, unlike the asbestos tiles downtown, stained with fifty-year-old cigarette smoke.

"Here you are, Detective. One sugar or two?" asked Officer Chen, who'd entered via the side door.

"No sugar, thanks. Or should I say, 'No thanks, sugar'?"

Joyce decided to forgo the exquisite pleasure of cracking her neck as she lowered it, fearing another lecture from her junior officer. Instead, she shrugged her shoulders and asked, "What do we know this morning?"

Raymond sat across from her and pulled his tablet from the special holder he'd created from ballistic fabric. Once he had some free time, he'd market it.

"I'll tell you what I know; you'll have to supply the rest."

"Okay, and thanks for the coffee, pal."

Raymond told her about his conversations with Mrs. Evans and Arlis.

"The report's on your laptop." He saw her hesitate, and moved closer to look over her shoulder. "No, not on your email and not on a text. Enter your password for the department's website. Joyce?"

"I've never tried to access it out of the office."

"So? Oh, I get it. The password is on a sticky note stuck to the desktop screen in your office. And now you want me to figure out how to sign you in." He moved back in front of her, the better to deliver a lecture.

"Well, you know what? I won't. I'm sick of you hotshots who think technology is someone else's job. You'd have a fit if someone blew your cover or took credit for an arrest, but you don't give a shit about data security.

"So get on the phone with tech support and figure it out on your own, sir." He sat down and stayed frozen in place until she finished making the call.

She wondered what had triggered this rare display of temper and gave him a long look. He seemed unusually tense.

Ten minutes later, she was looking at his report. She could have written Raymond up for insubordination, but decided to cut him some slack because she'd deserved the lecture. And she loved being called "sir."

"Okay. Let's set up some interviews."

Raymond unfroze and seemed to mentally shake himself back to his usual mild manner. "There's one of the three I think we should interview together—Ed Baxter, the new food bank board member. He seems a little shady. I wasn't able to track down Terry or Father Robert last night to get their input on this guy. They went to the hockey game in Mr. Monte's memory. I've put texts into them, but I'm guessing they're getting a late start this morning.

"Also no luck on finding the mysterious Mr. Jones, the one with the same last name as Lester. I'll wake Lester up in a while to see what he's found out."

"Lester?" Joyce asked. "Since when is he involved in this investigation?"

"Come on, Joyce, do you really think we could stop him? And I might as well tell you that Mae Perkins, the lady who discovered the body, is hanging out in the food bank line to see what she can find out."

"Just like the last murder," Joyce said, with a smile and a shake of her head. "You may remember that Daniel, the cute little organist, was the one who solved that one."

Raymond smiled too. "Yeah. All I had to do was put a hammerlock on the guy when he ran out of the church. So, now that we've covered what I know, what do you know, boss?"

Joyce told him about the press conference held yesterday afternoon just in time to make the evening news. "You won't believe this, but Chief Pierce fired back at the media on every stupid theory they had about the murder.

"No, it wasn't a homeless bum getting back at the rich folks living in the high rises. No, it didn't have anything to do with the murder here last spring. No, it wasn't a hardened criminal from the halfway house committing armed robbery for a hundred bucks."

Joyce had told the chief ahead of time what she knew about Nick's shady background, but he'd decided to hold off on the theory that his past had caught up with him until they had more information. That had also impressed her.

"And so I was able to get out of there in time to make my ladies' shopping and wine event."

To Raymond's "Huh?" she explained how women's clothing stores had started holding after-hours parties, helping the fashion-challenged to select and accessorize outfits to their heart's content, fortified by wine and appetizers.

"It was a blast, and they talked me into buying two outfits. Father Robert's Molly will eat her heart out when she sees this one. What do you think?" She stood up and moved to one side of the table.

Raymond looked up and froze.

Boom.

Chapter Eighteen

~~

THE WINDOWS RATTLED; THE old floor joists creaked. Joyce and Raymond locked eyes and then started running toward the front door of the parish hall, Joyce in the lead, Raymond radioing for backup. They turned left, ran past the old rectory, and then left again down the hill toward the source of the explosion.

They saw a smoking pile of what looked like old clothes just off the sidewalk at the entry to the food bank loading area. There didn't seem to be much damage other than some mangled cardboard boxes with bags of rice spilling out. There were no bodies on the ground—live, dead, or wounded. People were running toward the spot from all directions, but the only bystanders were two food bank volunteers standing in the doorway at the far end of the loading area.

Joyce ran into the building to check it out and evacuate the volunteers, and Raymond set to work securing the perimeter. He heard a knocking sound from up above and saw Arlis's face at the window of the food bank office, motioning to him. He waved back, signaling that he'd get to her in a minute.

Since the church, the old rectory, and the food bank were in the middle of the Central Seattle Precinct area, Raymond could track the sound of the sirens coming from every direction. It was truly ear-splitting when the noise from the cruisers coming uphill reverberated off the walls of the freeway underpass. He wondered if it was against procedure to insert earplugs on such occasions.

AT THE TIME OF the explosion, Robert and Terry were sitting in the hospital cafeteria across from Robert's condo, well out of earshot. The coffee was bad, but cheap; the breakfasts were cheap, but tasty.

All things considered, they weren't too hung over after last night's post-game wake for Nick. Their soccer buddies weren't heavy drinkers, since most of them started out as Nick's friends, not theirs, and Nick stuck to coffee or club soda.

"I felt a little guilty," said Terry, "egging them on to talk about Nick, but they didn't know any more than we do."

"I guess we should get back to Detective Joyce and tell her what little we do know," said Robert. "I grilled all my vestry members at the meeting yesterday and talked to the staff again. Poor Daniel; I think he's wearing the mantle of crime solver too heavily, after the case last spring. He kept saying, 'I know I heard something,' but has no idea what, or when or where. I told him to report to the officers anyway."

He continued, "I'm sure glad Dr. Lucy is head of the vestry this term. She won't stand for hearing a word said against Nick. Even Stacy's husband has backed off from forbidding her coming to the church. Which is good, because I need her help planning the funeral reception."

Terry put down his coffee cup in preparation to report on his board meeting, but Robert was on a roll.

"The Bishop is being a prince. We talked for half an hour this morning. I'm not one for praying over the phone, but he is, and I felt a lot better after."

Terry tried and failed again to talk.

"I was going to meet with him in a few days to officially ask for permission to marry Molly. Don't look at me like that; I told you how it is in the church. Anyway, he told me not to worry and that after this was over, we'd have a man-to-man over a glass of scotch in his office. That's one more thing I love about Molly. She's convinced him that I'm a cross between Bing Crosby in *Going my Way* and Carl Malden in *On the Waterfront*—"

Terry took no chances this time and started talking before Robert put the period on his last sentence.

"I called our warehouse manager; nothing's been missing from his side of the operation. Then I got on a conference call with the board. Our new member Ed Grafton was the only one who didn't know about the missing inventory. His take was it must be an inside job by one of the staff or volunteers. He also threw in that he took a dislike to Nick the minute he met him on Monday."

Just as Robert had done, Terry forged ahead, "I don't think he knows that the food bank's only employees are me and Arlis, and that our volunteers come from the same social level as the board. Can't you just see the volunteers from the churches and the Rotary Club and the high school kids doing community service being in cahoots to rob us blind?

"However," he barreled on, "I decided not to tell the board that Nick had in fact helped us out at the warehouse a couple of times. And wait! Now I remember; he was actually the first one to tell me we needed better inventory control. Said he'd never seen such a sloppy operation. Kind of hurt my feelings at first, but it kicked my butt into action.

"All the other jobs I've had, when something came up that required a lot of work, I'd just quit and take off on another trip. This time I didn't, and it was because of Nick."

Robert said, "So what if he did get involved at the warehouse? He helped everyone out. If there's something bad to find out about him, I don't want to be the one who finds it."

"Neither do I," said Terry, who was just regaining some energy after giving up the food stamp diet. Ever since Nick's murder, he'd been feeling weak, and now was no time to faint on the job.

Robert's phone rang.

"It's Arlis. You and Terry need to get to the church right now. There's been an explosion at the food bank." Her voice was loud enough for Terry to hear; despite his weakened condition, he shoved his chair back and sprinted out the door. Robert was two seconds behind him, and managed to run all five blocks without stopping to catch his breath.

Chapter Nineteen

~~~

Before the explosion, Deacon Mary Martin had been sitting in her office, filing her nails. There was nothing on her schedule. Last October at this hour she would have been at the Heritage House Retirement Community doing a Bible study or visiting someone in the nursing section, but now a conglomerate had taken over and built a second high rise across the street from Grace Church. This was not a house; it was a tower. They'd hired a chaplain for both sites who rigidly scheduled pastoral visitors.

Most of Puget Tower's residents were younger than she, having decided to settle down for good at age sixty. Why not? They had all the perks of condominium living, including a hermetically sealed view of Puget Sound and Mt. Rainier, a state-of-the-art fitness facility, access via van to shopping and cultural events, a four-star dining room, and separate suites for visiting family.

Mary and her husband Joe had moved to a condo themselves, so she understood the impulse. However, it bothered her that some of these younger elders shunned their compatriots needing the services of a walker or wheelchair, and complained when those compatriots wanted to use the main dining room.

She had to be fair; the "younger elders" were tireless volunteers. They were docents at the library and the museums. They helped out at their grandkids' schools, served on boards, and mentored their hearts out. They also volunteered at the Grace Church Food Bank and donated mounds of clothing and other items to the thrift shop.

Her mind wandered down the hill to the freeway. This time last year, she might have been underneath the I-5 Bridge, ministering to the homeless people who camped there. But her protégé Lester had taken that job over since he'd moved up a block into the old rectory. And even he complained that his charges were being gentrified out of the area. Their campground next to the freeway on-ramp had been razor-wired over, and the open-air feeding station nearby had been closed by the health officer.

Massaging her cuticles, Mary thought fondly of Father Robert's fiancée Molly, who had joined Grace Church after last spring's death in the Memorial Garden. Molly was now running interference between Mrs. Evans and Stacy Chase, the old and new guard of the churchwomen—a task that previously had fallen to her. And of course Father Robert had been spending every free moment with Molly or at soccer matches with Nick and Terry Buffett, instead of hanging out with Mary and her husband Joe.

Maybe she should retire and become a full-time grandparent? At least one of her five grandkids seemed to need her services at all times.

Worst of all, she didn't have anything to contribute to solving Nick's murder. Last spring, she'd been up to her eyebrows, defending Lester from the police who wanted to pin the crime on him and giving Daniel the support he needed to solve the mystery.

There was a knock at her door. The door was open, so she knew it was Daniel before he said, "Uh, Deacon Mary, can I come in?"

"Certainly, Daniel," she answered. "You can see that I have some free time."

"Oh no," said Daniel. "It's very important to keep your nails filed, because otherwise you could snag a finger on a piece of furniture—like an organ console, or even a keyboard. And that would upset your timing on whatever you were playing."

"I'll remember that, dear," said Mary. "But we can talk while I finish. What's up?"

Daniel sat on the puffy couch, which always seemed to decrease whatever anxiety he was feeling.

"Deacon Mary, Deacon Mary," he was crying, "someone else has died here at Grace Church."

She waited while he wiped his eyes and nose with the handkerchief she'd insisted he carry at all times.

Mary put her half-filed fingers to her heart. "I know, Daniel. It's one of the saddest things that's ever happened here. I didn't know Nick that well, and you probably didn't either, but we both know he was a wonderful man and didn't deserve to die like that."

"I feel so bad," Daniel said, "because I thought that once we discovered what happened when Ms. Clare died, it would never happen again. I thought that one time was enough."

"And since you were the one who found out who was responsible for Ms. Clare's death, I'll bet you think you're responsible for finding out who murdered Nick, too."

Daniel nodded forcefully. "That's right, I do. But I can't decide if I should try to help. If I do, then maybe another murder would happen, and then another."

Mary smiled. "I can understand that feeling. But Daniel, are you trying to say you have an idea about who killed Nick?"

"Well, I think I heard a clue when I was at the thrift shop on Monday. But I don't know what the clue was. It could have been a sound, or it could have been a time signature."

"Time signature?" asked Mary, bracing herself for a long explanation. Daniel tried to be concise. "The time signature is also known as meter. It's used in Western musical notation to specify how many beats are in each measure and which note value constitutes one beat. There's a lot more, but I'll stop there. The easiest way to describe it is like the beat of a drum."

"Okay, I get that," said Mary.

"Father Robert told me to talk to Detective Joyce, but I can't do that until I can name the clue. Do you have any advice for me?"

"Thanks for asking. My advice is to try not to think about it too much, especially at nighttime, when you need to sleep. Just tuck it away; that way it's more likely to pop into your head when you least expect it."

Mary had another idea. "Oh, and have you heard of arrow prayers? They're short prayers that you send up to heaven any time and any place. The best ones have just a few words like, 'Lord save me!' "

"Oh you mean like when I'm trying to master a new organ setting and I think *Help, help!* And then I've got it?"

"I guess."

Stacy Chase stuck her head in the doorway. "Deacon Mary, since Father Robert is away, can we go over the funeral plans for Nick with you?" She noticed the organist and said, "Oh hi, Daniel. Stop by the office later. Molly brought in some cookies."

Five minutes after Daniel left, Mary heard the explosion. She leapt to her feet, knocking over her manicure supplies. Pink polish oozed across the desk, but she didn't notice. She was already out the door on the way to the office. Mrs. Evans, Molly, and Stacy had dropped to the floor, thinking the boom was the beginning of an earthquake. Daniel was down there with them. Mary crouched down beside them and sent up an arrow prayer. Then she ran outside to check on the food bank volunteers. Thank heaven her schedule was empty today.

~~~

I'M STARTING TO ENJOY *this*, he thought. *Reminds me of the old days when I was establishing my territory. The old cronies would die of shock if they knew I was planning to set up on the grounds of a church. Once I'm done, this half block will be boarded up and I'll have bought it for taxes. Right up from the freeway, a few blocks from the wharf. Just what I need to set up shop. Too bad Dom won't be around to see.*

Chapter Twenty

~~~

"Don't ask me what I saw before the explosion," Arlis said to Raymond, when he arrived at her office. She was looking out the window and wearing the same gray sweater. "Ask me what I didn't see. I didn't see anyone lined up for the food bank. I look out the window a lot waiting for our crappy internet provider to give us some service."

And when you're talking to someone, Raymond thought.

"The line was there one minute and gone the next. They must have been warned, somehow. Oh good, Terry's here. And there's Father Robert, half a block behind him."

"Thanks, Arlis, this really helps," Raymond said, moving to her desk and leaning in between her and the window so she was forced to meet his eye. "I'll be around most of the day if you think of anything else. And here's my card."

On his way down the stairs, Raymond had an idea, based on what Arlis had said. Instead of figuring out who came out of the old rectory at the time Nick was murdered, they should try to find out who *hadn't* come out. He was almost certain that the killer had hidden in the building, unlocked the door to confuse them, and then left by another exit.

He was not surprised to see Mae Perkins outside the old rectory. She was becoming a fixture there.

"They told me the Ice Man is comin'," she gasped at him, winded from running. "All those folks at the bus stop back there." For a second Raymond thought she was talking about the play he'd struggled with in college, Eugene O'Neill's *The Iceman Cometh.*

"Slow down, Ms. Perkins. Who's *they* and who's the *Ice Man*?"

Mae looked him up and down. "You say you're a policeman and you don't know about the Ice Man? The one who sneaks up the street in his van and snatches up anyone who looks different from him? And *they*? They're the ones who were standing in the food bank line when someone came along and told them the Ice Man's comin'."

"You mean Immigration and Customs Enforcement, that ICE?"

Mae looked like she was going to spit on the ground, but she just shook her head and said, "So why does a devil who's setting off a bomb tell everyone to get out of the way, like he's a kind devil?"

"I don't think so, Ms. Perkins. I think he didn't want to hurt anyone, not this time." Raymond was thinking as he was talking.

"He just wanted to scare the sh—, I mean the cra— …. Anyway, ma'am, you know what I mean. He only wanted to scare away the people who come to the food bank and the thrift shop. He wants to scare away the volunteers too. He's trying to drive everyone away."

Mae nodded. "You're finally showing some sense, Officer Raymond."

Raymond knew he shouldn't. He'd never ask his granny to do it. But he said to Mae, "Ms. Perkins, I know Nick's murder won't stop people coming back to the food bank and thrift store. They need them too much. So if you still insist on going undercover, could you see if you could find out a few things?"

THREE HOURS LATER, FATHER Robert, Terry Buffett, Detective Joyce, and Officer Chen sat around the table in the Parish Hall eating takeout sushi. Deacon Mary had ordered it and was sitting quietly over by the piano.

"Deacon Mary, what are you doing over there?" said Joyce. "We need you here. I don't think the case earlier this year would have been solved without your keeping Daniel and Lester on track. And your husband solved the mystery of the buried box all on his own."

Mary walked over with a smile on her face.

The bomb squad had pronounced that the explosion was the result of setting off no more than two of the largest bottle rockets you could buy from one of the area's tribal reservations—meant to scare, not damage.

The group was looking at a creased floor plan of the old rectory circa 1935. It had been unearthed by Henry and spread across the middle of the table. That year the rectory had been moved one lot over from its original site, in order to accommodate a new parish hall. In the process the rectory had been rotated ninety degrees to the west, and a basement added. The full-length windows that had originally faced the Memorial Garden were now located two stories up and looked out over Puget Sound.

Each of the group also had a copy of a graphic Raymond had created detailing who was known to have gone in and out of the old rectory on Monday and the approximate times. Where possible, the names were accompanied by a recent picture, but there weren't many. He'd easily obtained pictures of the new food bank board member from Arlis but hadn't had much luck with the church members.

For instance, the only picture he could find of the organist Daniel was a long distance shot of him hunched over the piano in the parish hall. Deacon Mary had pulled that one out of the thick picture folder in her purse.

"Don't you post staff photos on your website, or your Facebook page?" Raymond asked Father Robert. He instantly regretted doing so. Father Robert looked done in. The word *haggard* came to Raymond's mind. It must have been one of the words that had lodged itself in his brain during college.

Robert mentioned the large cash donations in the collection plate, which might have been made by Nick. Terry mentioned the donations the food bank had received, but not the missing inventory at their warehouse. Detective Joyce, throwing caution to the wind, had filled them in on Nick's history in Canada, supplemented by Robert's recollection of his conversations with Nick.

Now Father Robert asked Joyce, "Would it help if I called the priest at Holy Trinity in Vancouver to see if he knows the name of the person who asked Nick to attend his relative's funeral?"

"Go for it," she said. "And since the church is on the seedy side of town, see if they know anything about the local syndicates, or know someone who does. Mention the name Joe Spano."

Robert took off his glasses and rubbed his eyes. "And here I thought the big item on my schedule this week was meeting with our Sunday School teachers." He stared up at the ceiling. "Nick, like I said, you owe me big time."

"By the way," he added, "we'd like to have his funeral on Friday. Can we go ahead?"

"You can," said Joyce. "The autopsy didn't take long; the cause of death was obvious and there were no drugs or alcohol in his system. He was a strong, healthy guy. And no one's contacted the coroner to claim the body."

Robert said, "All this started when Nick attended a funeral for someone whose relatives couldn't be bothered. But even though Nick didn't have any family, the church is going to be packed for his service."

Joyce stood and stretched her arms up over her head,

revealing a strip of trim waist. She slowly lowered them back down to her sides, making a whooshing sound. The others could only stare.

"Am I ever tired of sitting!" she said. "I've missed three yoga sessions so far this week. Just to let you know," she added, "Raymond and I will be there at the service, doing the cop thing to see who comes. It would be great if you could assign us some old-timers to help with ID's."

After his sprint from the hospital cafeteria to the food bank, not to mention the emotional toll of talking about Nick, Robert felt like a deflated balloon.

"Yeah, I know the drill from last spring. Your best bet is Dr. Lucy. She hasn't been here all that long, but she's made it her business to get to know everyone."

Raymond spoke up. "Mrs. Evans seems to keep an eye on everyone's business. Should we ask her too?" Seeing the others' less-than-enthusiastic nods, he added, "You can assign her to me, if you want."

BEFORE GOING BACK TO the condo to collapse, Robert stopped in at the office to check with Molly, Mrs. Evans, and Stacy on the funeral arrangements.

"Very good," he said, after reading the program for Nick's funeral. "And look at this drawing of Nick …. Where did you find it?"

Stacy said, "We worked on the program together. Mrs. Evans did the first draft and put in all the pertinent details."

Mrs. Evans added, "Mrs. Ferguson put on the finishing touches, describing Nick's many friends in the soccer and … ah … downtown community. And we printed all the verses of 'His Eye Is On The Sparrow' on the back."

"It's very fitting," said Robert, "but who—"

Molly jumped in, "Stacy chose the layout and added the details about the reception. We expect at least two hundred people at the service and another hundred for the reception."

"You're kidding," said Robert. I know Nick was likable, but his circle wasn't *that* big."

Stacy's blush extended well beyond her nose to include her ears. "Well, we managed to get some publicity in the press, and then the Sounders organization announced the funeral at last night's game. Don't worry, though. All of the food and drinks are donated. And I've made up some flyers about Grace church to hand out, so maybe we'll be able to welcome some new members."

Robert rubbed the top of his bald head. "But what about the picture?"

Molly and Mrs. Evans looked at Stacy. "The only picture of Nick was on his passport, and it's terrible. So Terry put me in contact with one of their Sounders buddies who's an artist, and *voilà*! Look, she even drew in the cross that he always wore. And … and … I've located someone who knew Nick. This person is paying her own way to the service and will be a surprise guest at the funeral and reception."

Molly, Mrs. Evans, and Father Robert all perked up. Stacy had withheld this information until now.

Robert said, "Stacy, it's wonderful that you've found one of Nick's friends, and I know that everyone will love to meet her. However, I'm sure you know that a funeral isn't like a TV game show. And since the service is on Friday, I'd like you to introduce me to the friend the minute she arrives, so we can do a little preparation."

Stacy hung her head. "Rick told me the same thing."

Chapter Twenty-One

~~~

DETECTIVE JOYCE WAVED A cup of coffee as she paced back and forth. "I'm tearing my hair out here, Raymond. It's Thursday, and the trail's not just cold, it's iced over. They've already assigned me two other cases. Pray that we get something at the funeral tomorrow."

"Pray? Really, Joyce, I'd rather not."

Raymond was glad he hadn't been pulled off the case altogether. He'd talked his sergeant into transferring him from foot patrol in the International District to the area near the church.

"Don't fret, Joyce, we're still in the research phase."

"Oh, Raymond, please. We don't need research; we need results."

"Here, I'm sending you the link to lawenforcementresearch. com. Cases with no known suspects, witnesses, or evidence have a horrible close rate, so no research, no results. I'm waiting for information on Ed Grafton, and I have a feeling we'll snag the elusive Mr. Jones. We're still looking for the guy who delivered water to the food bank on Monday. Now that I'm working under the freeway, Lester's homeless friends are willing to talk because he says I'm okay. And he's put the word out that if this case isn't solved, the food bank and thrift shop will go away."

Joyce checked the time. "Okay, partner. Who else do we need to interview before I have to go downtown?"

"We haven't talked to Daniel, the organist. He's our wild card. He says he heard something on Monday. And we need to re-interview Terry from the food bank. He was Mr. Monte's best friend and I think there's something he's not telling us. We need to get him away from Father Robert. I'll follow up with Arlis and Mrs. Evans on tracking down the water delivery guy."

"You like Arlis, don't you?"

"Yes, I do. I like many of my witnesses."

"I'll tell you who I like. That hunk of a Sounders player who stopped by yesterday to offer his condolences. He's got my card. Okay, let's march."

THEY MARCHED DOWN THE hall to Deacon Mary's office. Daniel had asked if she could be with him and if he could sit on her puffy couch to answer questions.

Mary welcomed Joyce and Raymond. They all sat in a circle around a table holding tea and cookies.

"I think it's best if you methodically take him through every moment he was in the thrift shop," Mary began.

One half hour later, Joyce and Raymond's ears were ringing. Raymond's notebook was filled with words like sonorous, thrum, and dissonance. They had also learned about time signatures.

On Monday morning the thrift shop had been a veritable hive of sound, at least to Daniel. He'd assigned one or two or three vocal characteristics to each person in the shop. Lucy was an alto with a well-modulated voice. Mae was a soprano who tended to talk right over pauses and periods.

"Mr. Nick was a baritone but could also go up in range to a falsetto. He tended to speak in 2:4 time. So, Detective Joyce and Officer Raymond, I think the clue I heard was either a tone or a time signature I didn't recognize. I have good hearing, so the sound could have come from some other part of the building. For instance, I know that the copy machine upstairs makes one copy every four seconds, which would be fifteen copies in one minute."

"So, Daniel," said Joyce, "if you remember this sound, or signature, or both, or hear it again, you'll let us know, right?"

"Yes, of course I will, but Deacon Mary and I have decided that I shouldn't think too hard about it." He looked at her. "I don't think they want to hear about arrow prayers."

Mary nodded.

JOYCE BRUSHED CRUMBS OFF her new tunic as they left the church. "Raymond, I've got to get to headquarters. Go ahead and talk to Arlis, and schedule a time for both of us to meet with Terry."

Chapter Twenty-Two

~~~

"WHY, MONSIEUR RAYMOND. *QUEL plaisir! Entrez, s'il vous plaît.*"

"*Gracias*, Mademoiselle Arlis, or is it Arlisse? The *plaisir* is all mine."

Raymond sat down and positioned his iPad. "Tell me again about seeing the water guy on Monday."

"So much for the pleasantries, I see. I never saw him. I just heard the bottles rattling."

"Does the same person usually make the delivery, and do they make it at the same time of day?" Raymond asked.

"Yes and yes."

"Does the delivery guy usually say something to you, or give you an invoice?"

"Yes and no."

"I'm not sure what's got you going, Arlis, but this is a murder case. I assume you want to find out who killed Nick."

Arlis started rocking back and forth. "So now I'm supposed to apologize and turn all cooperative. I really don't care who killed Nick; I just care that he's dead." She sighed and continued, "The water guy's name is Jeff—Jeff Mullins. He talks way too much, and Nick would usually run interference by coming up with him and staying afterward."

As she spoke, she rocked back and forth, back and forth.

"Is Terry around?" Raymond asked.

"He's down at the warehouse. He spends most of his time there since the thefts, making sure the new inventory control system is working."

"Thefts, you say?"

"Oh, *merde*! I guess he didn't tell you."

"So, how's the atmosphere been around here the past six months or so?"

"You mean since Nick showed up? And the thefts started?" She continued rocking and stared out the window.

After several minutes of silence, Raymond gave up and left.

As THE CHURCH LADIES had predicted, the pews of Grace Church were packed for the funeral. An honor guard of Seattle Sounders soccer fans in their team shirts served as ushers. Then they marched in procession behind Father Robert, Deacon Mary, the Grace Church choir and special guests, including Pastor Roxanne Washington of the neighboring Baptist church, whom Daniel had asked to solo on the anthem, "His Eye Is On The Sparrow."

Daniel had found every reference to sparrows in the Bible and the hymnal. The service bulletin included the portion of Psalm 84 that reads: *The sparrow has found her a house and the swallow a nest where she may lay her young.*

The cardboard box containing Dominic Monte's ashes lay on a small table in front of the altar, covered with a white linen cloth edged with embroidered crosses that Mrs. Evans had found in the sacristy. A huge floral arrangement sent by the Sounders FC stood nearby.

A contingent of people not comfortable inside a church gathered outside in the Memorial Garden. Lester acted as their unofficial minister, saying The Lord's Prayer and singing old-timey songs while accompanying himself on a thrift shop guitar.

All of Grace Church's vestry members attended and were assigned duties by Dr. Lucy. She reserved for herself the role of front door greeter, and was resplendent in a cream-colored suit and matching pumps. Around her neck was a tourmaline necklace donated to the thrift shop that Nick had persuaded her to purchase. Dr. Lucy handed out service bulletins and asked the mourners to sign the guest book. Detective Joyce, dressed in a basic blue suit, stood to one side.

Officer Raymond Chen, in a navy blazer and khaki pants, stood next to Mrs. Evans at the secondary entrance. Mrs. Evans was dressed in a black pantsuit and carried a notepad. Instead of whispering, which she felt was not acceptable in church, she communicated with Raymond in writing.

There was the usual holdup at the main entrance, as the mourners considered what to write in the guestbook—and in some cases, as with Nick's soccer buddies, what *not* to write. Some also hesitated over the address line. Dr. Lucy did what she could to speed up the process, saying, "Oh don't worry about that," or "Just write the name of your hometown."

A quick movement caught Joyce's eye as a man broke around the line and grabbed a program from the table, saying to no one in particular, "He didn't have any family, so what's with the book?"

The man was medium tall, balding, and wore a tailored gray suit. This made him stand out, since most of the mourners were customers at the food bank or thrift shop.

The man stalked off toward the front of the church.

"Who was that?" Joyce asked Lucy.

"I think he's the new board member at the food bank. I was at the thrift shop last Monday when Terry introduced him."

"Who else was with you, Lucy?"

"I'm sorry, Detective Joyce, but I can't talk right now."

Joyce walked to the other side of the church and pulled Raymond aside. Pointing to the man, she said, "Don't let that guy leave before we talk to him."

Raymond said, "That's Ed Grafton, the guy whose picture was in the food bank newsletter—the one that Arlis calls 'Mr. Thug.'"

"So we need to talk to him, but what we really need is someone who knew Mr. Monte from Canada. Check out the guest book and have Robert and Terry ask people at the reception."

Terry Buffett perched at the edge of a back pew. He hadn't mentioned his lack of religion when he applied for the job at the food bank. On a day to day basis, it hadn't been a problem. Father Robert wasn't one of those ministers who insisted that the price of a bag of groceries was being harangued with random Bible verses.

Other than giving the occasional talk at a church fundraiser, Terry hadn't darkened the Grace Church doors. Now here he was in a sports coat and a tucked-in shirt. He wasn't sure if he'd be turned away without a tie, so he was wearing a braided Western-style bolo.

~~~

ROBERT SPOTTED TERRY IN one of the back pews, looking ready to bolt. Now if he could just hold it together during the eulogy. Thank God Deacon Mary had reminded him about arrow prayers. He let one fly as he stood and walked up the stairs to the high pulpit.

"We're here today to celebrate the life of Dominic Francis Monte."

Robert pointed to the rear of the sanctuary and said, "Dominic, whom most of you knew as Nick, used to sit back there in what I think of as the 'Don't bother me' pews. His good friend Terry is sitting in the same section today. You may think that those pews are occupied by people not used to church who are a bit nervous and want a quick avenue of escape, but that's not entirely true.

"I've found that many of the 'Don't bother me' pew occupants are just shy. You know, Nick was really a shy man, despite his act at the thrift shop and his love of soccer."

Robert continued, "There's a point in our Sunday service where we stand up and greet the person next to us with the words, 'The peace of Christ be with you.' Now don't worry," he laughed. "We're not going to do it now.

"My point is that the folks in the 'Don't bother me' pews would rather be anywhere else right then. It was really hard for Nick, because people would make a beeline in his direction to shake his hand, or worse still, try to hug him. That's how well loved he was.

"Nick had perfected a few deflective moves. He'd slap the men on the shoulder. And you won't be surprised to learn that with the ladies, he'd lean over and plant a big kiss on their cheeks. That may seem pretty intimate, but it made the ladies feel wonderful and protected him from being hugged, which is what he feared.

"You see—and now I'm tearing up—Nick was a lonely man. I suspect that he went without hugs as he was growing up." Robert looked again toward Terry. "People tell me all the time that they're spiritual but not religious. These spiritual folks hardly ever darken the door of a place like this. It's as if they were afraid of being struck dead—either by God, who they assume is religious but not spiritual, or by hypocritical, holier-than-thou members. Or they're worried about being bored to death, which I admit is a real possibility."

Robert paused to wipe his eyes and his glasses, and then continued on what had become a rant. "I find that the spiritual but not religious are partial to movies showing ministers as real people who will sit with them in the back of a darkened church in their time of need. So at least they know to call for a minister when they're in the hospital or in big trouble."

"Tell it, Father!" Lester shouted from the front-row pew. A friend had saved him a place.

"Sometimes," Father Robert continued, "I think we should have a video monitor outside so people could see what's going on inside and realize that it's just a group of people using the rituals of their religion to practice being part of a loving, caring community, one that lets them experience awe at the poetry of the Bible and delight in the music that inspires them, whether it's the organ or a guitar. They also come to pray, and to gather strength for the week ahead. That's what I do, and that's what Nick did."

He stared at his notes and then looked up. "Friends, I find that I've come to an end. You're not going to hear me say what you might expect; that Nick is in heaven, kissing the cheeks of the angels. "The last thing I'll say I learned by reading Henri Nouwen, a Roman Catholic priest who was both spiritual *and* religious and lived in a community with mentally disabled people. They were his friends and companions, just as Nick was for us. When one of his friends died, he'd say, 'We've lost a companion, but gained a guardian.' We've lost a great friend in Nick, and gained a powerful guardian. Amen."

Pastor Roxanne led the mourners in singing "Amazing Grace," and then the ministers and others who had processed in processed back out just as formally.

During the service, Stacy Chase had been sitting with her husband Rick at the far end of a back pew, which would allow her to exit quickly to take care of last minute details for the reception. While Robert gave his eulogy, she stayed in place, frantically taking notes. She would have signs made for the 'Don't bother me' pews. She'd also check to see if a video camera could be installed at the church entryway to entice the spiritual but not religious. Father Robert was a marketing genius.

⚊⚊

AS PEOPLE WERE FILING out, Detective Joyce asked Dr. Lucy,

"Was there anyone you didn't recognize?"

"There were lots of people, but I know who he must be." Lucy pointed to a man in beige work clothes. "That's the person who delivers bottled water to the food bank once a week. I imagine that Nick formed a relationship with him, just as he did with anyone who came in the front door of the old rectory."

Joyce gave Lucy a thumbs up. "Mrs. Evans and Arlis both said the water guy was there the day Mr. Monte was murdered. It's good that he's here; otherwise it would be hard to track him down."

As Ed Grafton from the food bank board left the church, Joyce approached him and said, "We've been meaning to interview you, Mr. Grafton, and since you're here, we'd like to do it after you attend the reception."

She could see that he was preparing to let loose. "Now, Mr. Grafton," she said, "there's no need for that. You know we need to talk to you, because we've left numerous messages. So go in, say your hellos, perform your official duties and then we'll talk."

Chapter Twenty-Three

~~~

TERRY BUFFETT WAS MASTER of ceremonies at the reception. He felt much better overseeing a festive wake than attending a funeral. He invited people to share their memories, remembering Detective Joyce's request to ask where they were from and how they'd met Nick. Not surprisingly, everyone had met him in Seattle, and most declined to say where they were from.

Stacy had created an impressive memorial, which took up most of a long table. It featured the original of the drawing that had appeared in the bulletin, propped on an easel. Nick's Sounders shirt was also displayed, as well as one of his Hawaiian shirts. The crucifix he always wore was nestled in a velvet case. There were also a few of his favorite books. People viewing the memorial were surprised to see *The Confessions of St. Augustine* next to a selection of mysteries and thrillers.

Daniel had created an audio stream of Nick's favorite music. Vocal jazz predominated, along with Beatles classics, old school Doo-Wop, and Canadian performers Leonard Cohen, Joni Mitchell and Neil Young.

Catering had been provided by a culinary training program

for the homeless and paid for by donations solicited by Stacy.

After everyone had helped themselves to a plate of food, Terry called to the stage the mystery friend that Stacy had located. "I'm pleased to introduce Ms. Suzanne Burton."

Ms. Burton, dressed in a floral print dress, ascended the stairs to the stage, leaning heavily on the rail. She stepped up to the microphone. "I was Dominic's English teacher at Lincoln Central High School. Ms. Chase was so kind to contact me. It must have been difficult, because I've stayed away from the Internet.

"You nice folks have been too polite to ask me the question I know you're wondering. Of course, that is, was I surprised to learn that Dominic had been murdered? Now, I see some of you widen your eyes, as if that thought never crossed your mind."

She waited patiently until the murmuring stopped.

"I suppose the answer is that after seventy-five years of living, nothing surprises me anymore. As to what type of boy he was, he wasn't much different from the man you've described to me. And not much different from the typical teenage boy with a single parent, natural good looks, and athletic ability. He worked at a grocery store all through high school, and that's where he probably learned the customer service skills that you're all describing. He had a way with words, but wasn't so good at putting them on paper. Still, I see from your display that he developed a love of reading."

She continued, "Did he have a girlfriend, or was he inclined toward his own sex? I really don't remember. I don't remember if he went to church or not. And I'm sorry to say that I never met his mother. Parent-teacher conferences weren't so common in those days.

"I do remember how much everyone liked him, and how sorry they were when he moved away after high school and never returned. The reunion committees went to great effort to track him down, with no luck. I'll be able to tell his classmates that he eventually found a new home and a loving community."

There was fervent applause, and recollections of Nick continued for the next hour. Joyce kept an eye out for the hunky footballer, but he didn't show. She'd text him next week.

Chapter Twenty-Four

~~~

SINCE THE PARISH HALL was in use for the funeral reception, Joyce and Raymond interviewed Ed Grafton upstairs in a Sunday school room. They found some adult-sized chairs, but the table came to their knees.

Mr. Grafton took charge of the proceedings.

"Here's the deal," he said. "I'm at the funeral representing the food bank board. I didn't know Mr. Monte; the only time I saw him was Monday morning when Terry introduced us. I left the food bank office at eleven forty-five and went to lunch at my club. The manager can vouch for me. After lunch, I drove to our company warehouse in Tukwila, where I stayed until five. The warehouse manager can vouch for me. Now, what else do you want to know?"

Joyce had slicked her hair back for the funeral and now adopted her schoolmarm look. "Mr. Grafton, when you came into the church for the funeral, why did you say that Nick didn't have any family or friends? How do you know that?"

He shot back, "I made it my business to know that. Believe it or not, I'm supporting the food bank out of the goodness of my heart. And for me, that involves knowing the operation inside and out. Since Terry insists on having their headquarters in a broken-down church house that attracts every vagrant in the area, I asked around about this guy Nick who seemed to run the place."

"How often do you go to Canada, Mr. Baxter?" asked Raymond.

"What does that have to do with anything?"

"Since you've done all this research on Mr. Monte, you must know he moved here from Canada earlier this year."

"Sure I go to Canada. Like that's a big deal." Mr. Baxter reached into his pocket, drew out a wallet and pulled out a card. "See, here's my Nexus Pass. My mother lives in Richmond, south of Vancouver, and my company has a relationship with B.C. Trucking in the city. The last time I was up was Mom's birthday, which happened to coincide with our Labor Day. Even with Nexus, it took me four hours to cross the border."

"So you probably know Joe Spano," said Raymond.

"Nahhh, don't try to pull that on me. I know *about* Joe—who doesn't, in my industry? But I can guarantee you I've never met him."

Raymond made a note. "Perhaps with all your contacts, you can tell us how to get in touch with Mr. Spano?"

"So you think this Nick guy was part of Joe's crew? Well, I'll be damned. I didn't like his looks the one and only time I saw him." He put his wallet in his back pocket and stood up. "So, I'm thinking the police must have better things to do than trying to find out which crook killed another crook." He walked toward the door of the Sunday school room. "And that's all I'm going to say without my attorney present. Take my advice, officers, and move on."

After his departure, Raymond said to Joyce, "A worthy opponent, wouldn't you say?"

THEIR NEXT INTERVIEW, THE man from the water company, was sitting on a little chair outside the children's bathroom.

The patch on his shirt read Seattle Springs.

He stood up and extended his hand. "I'm Jeff Mullins. I've been working for Seattle Springs about five years. I started delivering to the food bank a year ago. Arlis got me set up after they found the water pipes were rusted. That's how we usually get the job. People think it's a luxury, but in situations like this, it's a necessity."

"Excuse me, Mr. Mullins," said Joyce, "can you wait until we get to the interview room?"

"All right. I do tend to ramble on." On the way, he did just that, "Nick loved the way I talk. He called it 'Jeff's monologues.' He'd tell everyone in the thrift shop to shut up and listen. Then he'd introduce me and I'd just start talking, telling him how my week had been. I live alone, so I take any chance I get to talk."

He sat down. "I told Nick he'd need to cut me off after five minutes or I'd be behind schedule. So when time was up he'd run his finger across his throat, like this. Then he'd help me carry the bottles upstairs to save time. He'd usually stick around to talk to Arlis." He dug into his pockets. "So anyway, here's my driver's license and passport."

Joyce put a finger to her lips, and Mr. Mullins paused. "So, you have a passport? Where do you travel?" She paused so he could answer.

"It's just a precaution, really, in case I ever decide to go to Canada. I'm a dog lover, and they have some of the best shows."

Raymond asked, "So, did Nick have you do the monologue the day he was killed?"

"What day was that? I make my deliveries on Tuesday. But I got turned away this Tuesday because of it being a crime scene."

"Who turned you away?"

"Lester, the night watchman, and his dog Spike. How about that Spike? What a specimen of the breed. And Lester? You want to talk about monologues. That guy has us all beat."

Finger up.

"You mean you didn't make a delivery on Monday?"

"No, like I said, Tuesday's my day for this part of town."

Joyce asked, "Is there any chance someone else from the company came on Monday?"

"I suppose anything's possible, but the owners are pretty stingy about granting special requests. Maybe Arlis made a request I didn't know about. The dispatcher likes her. Well, I like her too, and so did Nick. So maybe they made an exception. Anyway, I was sure sorry to hear he'd been murdered, and if there's any way I can help you, just let me know."

Joyce stood up and handed him her card. "I do think you can help us, so I appreciate the offer. We'll be in touch."

Chapter Twenty-Five

~~~

MOLLY FERGUSON AND ROBERT Vickers sat at one of the round tables in the parish hall. People were cleaning up around them. Nick's funeral reception had wound down, and the only people remaining were a few stalwart members of Grace Church and some street people enjoying the last of the sandwiches and cookies.

Molly had kicked off her shoes and Robert had torn off his white clerical collar. He now looked more like a New Age sage than a Christian minister.

"Robert, I've never seen you take off your collar on duty. Are you ill?" Molly reached over and felt his forehead. It was cool and sweaty.

"I'm exhausted," Robert said in a flat voice. "I don't think I've ever felt so exhausted. It's scary. I don't think I can move."

Molly waved away a church elder who was coming up to talk, hoping they wouldn't be too antagonized. She also hoped she wasn't revealing how worried she was. That worry would spread around the room in five seconds.

"Let's go," she told him. "I'll tell people you have a meeting with the detectives. Robert, you have to stand up on your own. It won't do to have me supporting you."

She spotted Terry and waved him over.

"Terry, just sit down next to Robert and say any old thing to him."

Terry did as he was told, saying, "Robert, you look like shit."

"Now, reach under the table and grab him around the waist. Get him upright and march him out of here to his office. I'll run interference."

No one seemed to notice the maneuver, and in a few minutes, Robert was seated in the big, comfy chair in his office designated for visitors, and Terry was bringing him water and a wet paper towel for his forehead.

Terry looked at Molly. "Should I call the aid car?"

"No!" said Robert.

"Terry, you need to get back out there," said Molly. "If anyone asks, tell them Robert's in a meeting with the detectives. I'll text you."

After fifteen minutes, a big glass of water, and the undivided attention of his beloved, Robert felt better.

"Remember last spring when we sat in front of the fireplace and roasted marshmallows? That was when I knew I wanted to marry you. And have I mentioned yet how beautiful you look right now, especially in that red—"

"You need to take some time off." Molly answered.

"No."

"Yes. You don't have a choice, because I'm telling the bishop. I'll tell him to say he insisted you take a few days off. He doesn't have anything on his schedule this Sunday, so he can take your services. And then next week you're going to see your doctor. I'm worried about your blood pressure.

"Molly, are you going to order me around for the rest of our lives?"

"Until death do us part," she said, "but only when you act

as perverse and foolish as you're acting now. And those words come straight from the Bible somewhere. If and when I act perverse and foolish, you can order me around, too."

Chapter Twenty-Six

~~

"THE LORD BE WITH YOU!"

As Molly had promised, Bishop Anthony Adams was at Grace Church for both Sunday services. Daniel made sure that the bishop's mic was disconnected, knowing from experience that his decibel level was too robust to require amplification from the Grace Church sound system.

Bishop Anthony began the sermon in the traditional way, commenting on the scripture readings for the day. But after ten minutes he moved from interpretation into exhortation.

"Father Robert lost a parishioner this past week, and I ordered him to take today off. Now, some of you may think that your rector was too close to Dominic Monte, a man from out of town—a new member of the congregation with no visible means of support. Perhaps you felt that this friendship would take away from the time Father Robert could devote to the smooth operation of Grace Church or," he jabbed a finger, "to you, or you, or you!"

He paused for what seemed like an hour.

"Well, let me tell you what I think. I think that there are people who come into all of our lives who have something special to teach us. We don't know when they'll arrive, and they don't arrive often. And I think that Mr. Monte was that person, not only for Father Robert, but for all of you as well."

The bishop continued, "Now you may be wondering, what's so special about a new parishioner who decides to do a lot of volunteering and takes your rector to soccer games?

"What's so special? You tell me.

"Tell me the weekly golf games I enjoy with my friends aren't important. Ask my wife Betty; she's down there in the second row. Ask her what a guy like me with a Type A personality would be like to live with if I didn't have the golf games, and yes, the beers after.

"And tell me, folks, that you'd gladly give up your ladies' nights out and your Super Bowl Sundays.

"What did Nick teach Robert? He taught him the value of camaraderie, friendship if you like. That's made him a finer person, and yes, a better pastor to you.

"THANKS BE TO GOD!"

Chapter Twenty-Seven

M ONDAY MORNING AT 6 a.m., Joyce was awakened by the beep announcing a text message. The words on her phone's screen read, "Got Mr. Jones!"

She and Raymond arranged to interview him at the church, hoping Jones would be more forthcoming at the scene of the crime. Two of their fellow officers picked him up at the jail and waited during the interview.

When Mr. Jones was seated across from her, holding a cup of church coffee, Joyce took a chance. "So, you're the Mysterious Mr. Jones who set off the bottle rockets last Wednesday. Were you paid to kill Dominic Monte, too?"

Mr. Jones was shivering in his jail jumpsuit. He was a slender man, about forty, and still had a full head of wavy black hair. "I didn't kill Dom! And if someone told you I did, that means I was framed."

"You call him Dom; you knew him," said Joyce.

Mr. Jones said nothing.

"So tell us about the bottle rockets," said Raymond.

"You have no proof I did it."

You're right on that, Joyce thought.

To her delight, he continued, "But if I did, it would be because someone offered me quite a bit of money to do it. But that person would have made his offer through intermediaries."

"Like maybe Ed Grafton of Grafton Trucking?" asked Raymond.

Mr. Jones said nothing.

"Or Joe Spano, from Canada?" asked Joyce.

Nothing.

"Now we're going to reacquaint you with a couple of people," said Joyce, waving her arm.

Lester and Mae came over from the corner.

"So, Lester, I'd like you to identify Mr. Jones as the person who threatened Mr. Monte on the day he was murdered."

"I can't do that, sorry, Detective Joyce," said Lester. "It wasn't this man; it was someone else. However, I can verify that I have seen this man hanging out at the freeway entrance. And you know I have." Lester glared at Mr. Jones. "Don't try to deny it."

"I'm not denying it," Mr. Jones said with a smile. "But as you just said, I'm not the one who threatened this guy that got himself killed."

"So, Mae," asked Joyce, "was this the person who got into a ruckus at the thrift shop?"

Mae's disgust was palpable. "No, this isn't him, and if you police can't do a better job of finding Nick's killer, I'll haunt you all after I meet my Maker."

~~~

MONDAY MORNING, AFTER HIS enforced Sunday vacation, Father Robert sat slumped over his desk. He was remembering the visit that Bishop Anthony, the bishop's wife Betty, and Molly had made to the condo yesterday after the services. First in the door, Bishop Anthony reassured him that the congregation was none the worse for wear after learning that their rector wasn't up to his Sunday duties. Betty and Molly followed with orange juice, champagne, a fruit plate, and assorted bakery delicacies, all purchased at Foodie Market.

BISHOP ANTHONY LOVED SOCIAL gatherings, and debriefed him about the morning in detail. "If I do say so myself, people like to see their bishop, and I was able to reassure your folks that this murder wasn't a sign from on high that Grace Church was doomed. I told your little organist to end with 'A Mighty Fortress is our God'—just the thing to lift their sprits."

Robert said, "He didn't give you ten reasons why that hymn was all wrong for the season?"

"He started to open his mouth," said the bishop, "but all I had to do was lift my crozier, and he thought better of it. And Mary, that deacon of yours … what a gal. After the service she was working the room like a pro, offering reassurance and hugs."

Robert nodded and said, "My spies tell me that attendance was on the light side." He'd asked Dr. Lucy to call him with a report.

"Stands to reason," said Bishop Anthony. "Most of them had been to your deceased's funeral on Friday, and probably thought that would do it for the week. Besides, they didn't know I would be there."

He looked around the condo's living room. "Betty, don't you wish we'd had a nice little place like this when we were starting out? Remember the rectory in Missoula? How the oil tank would go dry during a blizzard and the mosquitoes would descend like the plague in summer?"

He drained his glass and got up. "Got to get home to childproof the house before the grandkids arrive. Robert, my advice to you is to take it easy, let the police do their jobs, and let your deacon calm the waters. Pretty soon everything will have settled down.

"Oh, and don't forget to make an appointment so I can grill you about your qualifications to marry Ms. Ferguson here." He laughed. "Just kidding."

Robert felt his blood pressure rise twenty points. He opened his mouth to admonish his bishop that Nick's life was worth more than a blip on the church's radar. That at the very least this second murder on sacred ground in one year required the full commitment of the church staff and leadership to retake that ground.

The look on Molly's face would have stopped a train going full speed. Her amber eyes, set off by long auburn lashes, seemed to be sending out little lightning bolts. So Robert swallowed instead and said his goodbyes. After the Bishop and Betty left, Molly went to the hall closet, saying, "Let's get our coats and take a walk."

After they descended the three flights of stairs to the street, she said, "Robert, I was serious Friday when I said you need to see your doctor. I know how upset and angry you are, but think of the consequences if you'd unloaded on the bishop just now."

He took a few breaths. "You're right. I know that I need a medical tune-up, and I'll get one. And bless you for stopping me from blowing up at the Bishop. And by the way, the facets that sparkle off your eyes when you're mad … oh, my!" He smiled, then added, "But Molly, I made a commitment to Grace Church when I first came that I wouldn't let the church die on the vine and be sold from under our feet. We managed to survive Clare's death, and repairing the church tower is just the first step in rehabbing the sanctuary. After that, we can decide the best use for the old rectory and gym. None of this would have happened if we hadn't all come together to make it happen."

They'd reached the top of First Hill and the plant-filled entrance to Seattle University. "This time someone is trying to turn our church block into a battlefield, to scare us away. We can't just hope, like the bishop says, that it will blow over."

Molly thought for a moment before answering. "You know, Robert, the circumstances of Claire's death were different. She wasn't murdered in cold blood. Nick's killing is on whole new level. It involves criminal elements from outside of the church. This really is a police matter."

Robert waved his arms. "I know that. I know that. But it doesn't mean that we can't help the police and make sure they don't give up. Detective Joyce will be back at headquarters tomorrow and we need eyes on the ground around the church. Heck, I couldn't stop Mae and Lester and the others even if I wanted to."

They had walked a few more blocks by now, and could see Lake Washington ahead. Robert was puffing and Molly had taken off her scarf.

"Let's head back," he said. "I don't have anything official to attend tonight, so maybe you can help me draft answers for the bishop when he grills me about our getting married."

Molly pointed him to a bench in the nearby pocket park.

~~~

ROBERT RAISED HIS HEAD off the desk, stood up, and walked to Deacon Mary's office. It was empty, except for a steaming cup of tea. He dropped onto to her puffy sofa and waited.

After pouring him a cup of tea and listening to the first part of his account, Mary asked, "What did Molly tell you when you sat down in the park?"

"She told me that she loved me and wanted to marry me. She told me that about four times. But then she said that we shouldn't announce our engagement until I was back on an even keel. An even keel!" He threw up his arms. "She wants us to go on like we have been, just put off the wedding plans. Like a fool I told her that in that case I'd rather not see her for the time being. Mary, I need to talk to Joe and ask him why I said such a stupid thing. I know I can take it back, but I need to know why I told her that, even though it was stupid. After Clare died last spring, I asked him some similar questions, and his answers really helped."

Mary shook her head and said, "Robert, you know that Joe would be glad to talk to you. Actually, he's been missing the talks you had last spring, and he was so pleased to be involved in that investigation. But then—"

Robert broke in, "When it was all over and the church was back on a so-called even keel, I just dropped him, didn't I? I fell in love with Molly and fell in with Terry and Nick and the soccer games and all that, and I forgot about both of you." Robert threw up his hands, which seemed to be a new habit. "That's another reason I need to speak to you both, not just Joe. My God, couldn't I realize that you don't have to give up your loved ones when you add new ones?"

"Robert, would you like to come for dinner tonight? Joe has to tend to his beer barrels afterward, so you can talk to him at his home-brew club while he's fiddling with the dials and such."

"I'd love to, Mary. And I'm going to call Molly to brief her on my first effort to get back on that even keel."

AFTER ENJOYING A DELICIOUS meatloaf dinner, Robert walked with Joe to the brew house two blocks away. Residents of the downtown condos had many such communal spaces where they could pursue projects that would ordinarily require an onsite garage or shop.

"The secret's in the hops, Robert. Lucky for me the best quality product is grown right over the mountains in the Yakima Valley. And I have an inside line on a supplier who's willing to deal in small amounts. If I was more ambitious, I could set up a syndicate." He laughed. "That makes me sound like a drug dealer, doesn't it?"

Robert felt his eyes burn with fatigue as Joe pointed to various brewing components. He loved a nice glass of beer, especially the Belgian ale brewed by the monks, but decided to move the conversation toward the reason for his visit.

"Joe, I have to say you're a lot more relaxed now than you

were last Spring when you helped us out with the Memorial Garden mystery."

"You know, you're right," Joe replied. "I was glad to help, but I didn't like the pressure to perform. Maybe it has something to do with brewing beer, but these days I'm finding it easier to focus on what's right in front of me instead of what's around the next corner."

"That's it, Joe. That's what I want to be able to do." Robert paused, trying to think through what Joe had just said.

"I want to know how to live through today and tomorrow and the days after that without obsessing over who killed Nick. And what the future holds for Molly and me. And … what the future holds for Grace Church."

Joe asked, "Why does it bother you so much not knowing who killed Nick?"

"That's easy. It offends my Old Testament sense of justice. I want my eye for an eye. Plus, it happened on my patch, so I feel responsible."

"And what was wrong with telling Molly you want a time out?

"I feel like I don't deserve her, so I'm giving her the chance to pull out all together. I know I can take back what I told her, except I don't want her to think of me as an indecisive wimp."

Joe laughed as he extracted a shot glass of beer for each of them. After the toast, he said, "I think you may have a deeper reason for needing a time out. I don't know what it is, but I wouldn't decide too quickly on that one. And do you really think you can predict what the future holds for Grace Church?"

"I know what I want it to be."

"What's that?"

"Well, I guess I want it to keep all the beauty that draws people in to pray, but also be strong enough not to fall down on them when the big one hits. I want it to be a gathering place for the whole community, not just the rich or just the poor, for all ages, for animals, visiting tourists, the mayor … you get the picture. A place where people can feel safe. I could go on and on."

After a few more minutes of conversation, Robert clapped Joe on the shoulder. "Great beer, and great advice. And you're right, I do need a break."

It had started to rain. They put on their parkas and hoods and walked the two blocks back to Joe and Mary's condo.

THE NEXT MORNING, AFTER making an appointment with his doctor and emailing Molly to let her know, Robert set out on a walk, retracing the route he'd taken with Molly. He stopped at the park bench to eat a sandwich and reflect on his life so far.

First he recalled his youth in rural Montana as the youngest in a well-adjusted, church-going family. He smiled, remembering how he refused to go to Sunday school, preferring instead to stare at the stained-glass windows and address his theological questions directly to the pastor.

His parents affectionately described him as the most stubborn and idiosyncratic of their kids. He began collecting *Mad* magazines in grade school and had never stopped. He drove his teachers crazy with unanswerable questions, and they allowed him chunks of time in the library for "independent study."

In high school his miserable eyesight kept him out of sports, but the football team adopted him as their "trainer," and he learned how to wrap ankles with the best of them. His letter jacket was still in the closet.

He met his ex-wife at college. Her level of idiosyncrasy matched his; Sandy was obsessed with moths and butterflies and had a huge collection. They married after graduation and moved to the Bay Area so she could study medicine and he could study theology, with the goal of becoming a teacher or chaplain.

Then, assigned to a parish in San Mateo for an internship, he realized that he much preferred the role of minister. He could now be a "spiritual trainer." The older church members indulged his enthusiasm; the members his age "adopted" him, and the little ones knew he was a child at heart.

Sandy had been at best a C and E churchgoer, which meant she only attended at Christmas and Easter. Robert had no objection to her continuing on this schedule, but she resented his role in the limelight on Sunday mornings, also the late night calls—even though she certainly received her share.

Robert had been distraught when she filed for divorce, but knew now that neither of them had been mature enough at the time to work it out.

As he sat on the park bench and finished his apple, he realized something for the first time: for over twenty years now, he'd avoided romance and marriage by becoming over-involved in church activities. His few serious relationships had foundered because he'd been unable to transfer enough time, devotion, and commitment from the congregation to an individual. But now he knew that if he matched his stubbornness and maturity with Molly's, all would be well—better than well.

His healthy lunch had not begun to satisfy his appetite, and after stopping for fish and chips, he walked to the northbound freeway entrance below Grace Church. No amount of gentrification would prevent this spot from being a boundary area, home to the troubled and transient and also a throughway for their more prosperous neighbors to their downtown offices.

The public hospital to the south of the church would continue its mission to serve the destitute, despite the condominium towers and trendy businesses that had sprouted up around the church block. Grace Parish would continue to be vulnerable. There was nothing he could do about that. But he wouldn't want to be stationed anywhere else.

Chapter Twenty-Eight

～～

THE CITY WAS RUMBLING to life early Tuesday morning as Mrs. Evans unlocked the front door to the old rectory. Light had been bothering her eyes, so she didn't turn on the overhead fluorescents. She stopped in the foyer and stared at the counter for a long time, the counter where Nick had died.

She'd been so proud when the thrift shop opened. At her insistence, all the donations had been cleaned, restored to decent condition, and priced reasonably. She'd refused to sell used underwear, asking Terry to tap his food bank suppliers for what he called "new product" at bargain rates. If the food bank could use cash donations to buy paper towels, large bags of rice, flour, and other items that weren't likely to be donated, then why couldn't she use the profit from sales of thrift shop collectables to buy new underwear?

The down and out and the collectable buyers had gotten along for the most part, and she knew that Nick had been responsible for the upbeat atmosphere. Why had she given him such a hard time?

Because she'd been afraid of him. His physicality, his eyes that wouldn't let yours go, his ability to cut through all of your defenses—defenses you'd spent your life building and hiding behind. His invitation to step outside your skin and follow him without asking where.

The people at church thought she was heartless, but it simply wasn't true. Nick knew she had a good heart.

Most of them didn't know she'd been a social worker before she married. And now she couldn't remember why she hadn't told them. During her studies she'd learned about the settlement house movement. In the early 1900s, especially in Chicago, benefactors bought large homes located in what had become slums—slums that housed newly arrived immigrants from all over Europe. They converted them to community gathering places, providing education, basic services, and a refuge from the hardships of life in the tenements.

Call them ladies-bountiful if you wished, teaching hygiene and table manners to the unwashed, but these pioneers had conducted the first demographic studies of poverty and lobbied tirelessly for reform. She would have loved to be one of them. Instead, born many years too late, she'd married, resigned her job, had two children, and relocated with her husband to Seattle. She'd had a satisfying life raising her children, volunteering, and serving her church. A satisfying life, but not a trailblazing one.

Along the way, she'd searched the church archives and learned that Grace Parish itself had provided ministry to ladies of the night and their children in the 1910s and 20s. Then, in the 1960s, church leaders had converted an old hotel they owned across the street into a halfway house for released prisoners. They'd also developed a thriving Sunday school for children in the nearby public housing development.

In the 1970s the Grace Church gym, which had formerly been the scene of inter-church basketball games, had been converted to a food bank. Having discovered this, she'd been eager to expand the church's mission into the 21st century.

Now, looking at the deserted thrift shop space, her heart

sank. Even a thorough cleaning and tidying couldn't disguise what it was: cramped, dusty, and stuffed with castoffs. An unbidden thought sunk her spirits further. In her drive to expand her territory, she'd driven the rector of her church out of his rightful home, a home he loved.

She walked to the counter, steadying herself against the various racks and shelves. The police had searched the cash register and retrieved the envelope containing Monday's receipts, but she decided to take another look. There was no cash in the drawer—she hadn't expected that—but it wasn't entirely empty. In the few months the shop had been open, it had already collected the usual bits and pieces.

She was tempted to put on a vinyl glove, but decided to throw caution to the winds. Her searching fingers flicked forward paperclips, a toothpick, and a few scraps of paper. She put everything on the counter and then rubbed the drawer clean with one of her eyeglass wipes.

There was writing on both scraps of paper. Officer Chen might want to look at these; he had an eye for detail. She'd call him. Not the detective. She'd use the wall phone.

Where was her purse? There, on the chair. Everything seemed so blurry. She fumbled inside the purse until she felt the edges of Officer Chen's card. She'd transferred it to her purse from her desk. Now, if she could just read the number and punch the right buttons ....

~

RAYMOND'S CELLPHONE CHIRPED. HE was sleeping in on his granny's couch, after escorting her home from a family party. There was no one on the line, but the prefix was local. He used the reverse directory and verified that the call came from the thrift shop. He called for an aid car and radioed for a ride, ASAP.

When he burst through the door of the thrift shop ten minutes later, the aid crew was bent over someone lying behind the counter. Lester was sitting on the floor nearby holding his head. Spike leaned against him.

Raymond edged in beside the crew and saw that it was Mrs. Evans. She squinted up at him and mumbled, "Look on the counter, Officer, at the pieces of paper … writing on them. Might be important? Eye for detail … hope you …." One of the crew placed the oxygen mask over her mouth.

"Stroke?" Raymond asked.

"Looks like it," answered the paramedic.

Raymond moved over to Lester and said, "It's okay, man. They'll take good care of her. Can you call the church folks and tell them Mrs. Evans will be at Harborview Hospital? I'll be in contact."

Lester rubbed his face and nodded. "Spike and I have witnessed more bad things in one month at this old rectory than we did on the street in the past five years."

After everyone left, Raymond swung into action: bagging the pieces of paper, radioing in to the station, briefing a groggy Joyce, putting on his gloves, and searching the area behind the counter.

He made an executive decision not to dust for prints. The area had been dusted after Mr. Monte's murder and even if someone had planted the pieces of paper later, Mrs. Evans's prints would obliterate everything else.

Now he could take a look at what was on the papers. He didn't expect much. Mr. Monte wouldn't have had time to do anything before the bullet hit him, even assuming he knew who the killer was.

God, he hoped this was Mr. Monte's writing, because the same three names were on both pieces. And Raymond recognized the names. It looked as though Nick had been arranging them into some sort of diagram, hadn't been satisfied with his first effort, and had switched to the second scrap of paper. Raymond called Joyce back, and they arranged to meet in half an hour.

Chapter Twenty-Nine

~~~

"FATHER VICKERS? THIS IS Morris Whalen, from Holy Trinity Parish in Vancouver. I'm sorry to be so long returning your call; I was out of town on family business."

Robert smiled into the phone. It always gave him a lift to speak to a colleague. They exchanged pleasantries and information ("How large is *your* congregation? How do you get along with *your* bishop?") for a few minutes.

"I was sorry to hear about Dom's death," Morris said. "He was a good man, and was a big help to us during his time here. Besides the church, we have three low-income housing buildings, a soup kitchen, a drop-in center, and a job-training program. He came every day with his tool kit and did all sorts of repairs. He also helped keep order at the drop-in center."

And here Robert had thought Grace Church had a lot of programs …. He told Morris, "Nick's domain here was the thrift shop located in our old rectory. But Morris, I notice you refer to him as Dom. He was always Nick to us."

"Interesting. All I can think is there's a big European presence in Vancouver. Anyone named Dominic is automatically called Dom."

Robert mentioned the Seattle Police Department's interest in Joe Spano and his organization, and asked if Morris was familiar with them. Morris was.

"I've lived in this part of town for years, and the Spano name is well known. The family attends the Roman Catholic Church, so I haven't met any of them personally. Dom told me he was in the process of extricating himself from a criminal organization, but I don't know if it was Spano's."

He continued, "I know that Joe is the patriarch of the family, and I'd guess he's nearing eighty. You don't hear his name much anymore; his son has assumed control."

Robert sighed. "Nick probably told you what he told me—that he never knew his father. No wonder it was hard for him to break away, no matter who ran the syndicate."

"He did tell me," Morris said, "and of course you're right. If it was Spano's group, I wonder how Dom and Spano's son got along? When he decided to head south, Dom told me it was best that he make a clean break. He was lucky to have dual U.S.-Canadian citizenship.

"But you know, Robert, I had the impression he was headed farther away than Seattle. He mentioned Los Angeles. I gave him the name of a church there that I was sure would welcome him."

Robert said, "If only he hadn't stopped in Seattle and found Grace Church. But I can understand. When you lose the ones you consider to be family, the longing for a spiritual home can overwhelm your instinct for self-preservation."

"You're so right. Robert, I've really enjoyed our conversation. Let's try to arrange a visit."

THE ST. FRANCIS DAY animal blessing a week later was a subdued occasion. Even Stacy's enthusiasm had been depleted by Nick's murder and Mrs. Evans's stroke. She'd dropped her plans for a chaotic inside-the-church service, relocating the event to its usual location, the Memorial Garden. The outline of the square of lawn that had received Nick's ashes was still visible. Although there were no plaques or identifiers allowed, a fresh flower had been placed in that square each day since Nick's funeral.

When he saw the red rose, Father Robert's spirits, which were much lower than Stacy's, flapped their wings and rose a bit. He remembered other efforts by friends and family to personalize their loved one's patch of grass: tiny American flags, pictures in waterproof bags, baseball caps. Sooner or later, the efforts ended; he hoped it was because the garden itself created its own memorial, lined as it was with flowering plants and blessed with the feet of children hunting for Easter Eggs and the paw prints of animals being blessed on St. Francis Day.

Spike sat right on top of Nick's plot, rose and all, when he wasn't welcoming members of the animal congregation and their owners. Standing off to the side, Lester strummed his guitar.

"Father Robert!"

Robert looked up to see a parishioner standing on the deck of the high-rise retirement community across the street. His spirits fluttered higher when she dangled her cat over the balcony so he could bless it from afar.

Five minutes later, Robert's spirits departed when, in a misguided attempt to cheer him up, Terry lifted up a carry case containing a toy snake, knowing that his friend was terrified of reptiles of any kind. Since Robert hadn't washed his glasses, he mistook it for the real thing. His scream could be heard two blocks away.

~~~

ARLIS STOOD IN THE Memorial Garden holding the case occupied by her Siamese cat Voltaire. She cringed when she saw Spike sitting on the perfect red rose she'd left earlier for Nick.

Voltaire received his blessing from the traumatized Father Robert with a Gallic hiss. Ordinarily Arlis would have left immediately, but found herself enjoying the camaraderie of the other pet owners. And Lester wasn't half bad on the guitar. She was one of the last to go, pausing to revive Nick's rose on her way out of the garden.

Rounding the corner to the front of the parish hall, she saw Stacy Chase standing in the middle of the sidewalk, holding a tissue to her bright red nose. Arlis started to back away, but was stopped in her tracks by an unbidden thought: *What would Nick do?* She forced herself to move forward.

It turned out that Stacy had planned a second event for that afternoon. In a few minutes' time, Father Robert would go from animal blesser to baby blesser, conducting a baptism inside the church. The baptism would be followed by a party in the parish hall. Arlis and Stacy stood side by side and watched through the window as a giant rubber playhouse was inflated inside. Stacy's strategy was to provide a post-baptism party with all the bells and whistles to attract as many friends, family, and children as possible. She'd even designed a smash cake in the shape of a dove for the baby to destroy, figuring that no one would worry too much about the bad symbolism. The word was spreading that beautiful, historic Grace Church was family friendly.

Stacy snuffled, "It's been a year and a half since Rick and I were married, and I'm afraid I'll never have a baby to be baptized. And what if he wants to divorce me if we can't have children? And … and … I'm an only child, and if I don't have a baby, there will be no one to carry on the Upton name."

Arlis thought, but didn't say, *Have you tried a cat*? Instead she said, "Stacy, Stacy, shhhhh … everything will be okay. I know it will."

After a few more exchanges in this vein, Stacy was calmer. She squinted her eyes at Arlis and asked, "Who does your hair?" Before Arlis could answer, she said, "Your last name is Bell. Are you a Bell descendant?"

Arlis began nudging Voltaire's cage up the sidewalk. "Well, yes, my last name is Bell, so I guess that makes me a descendant."

"No, I mean a descendant of one of the founding families of Seattle, like my family," said Stacy. "I can find out in a few minutes." She drew an iPad out of her purse. "Tell me your parents' and grandparents' names."

What would Nick do? Arlis thought again.

Just tell her.

So she told Stacy what she remembered, and it took Stacy all of five minutes to verify that she was indeed descended from the Seattle-founding Bells.

"So, Arlis, it's like we're sisters," Stacy said. "And … and … together we can put this old church back on the map."

~~~

I've cut myself off from the family, but who cares, anymore? Mom and Pop are long gone. Theresa is gone, two years, now. The sisters and daughters all married outside the clan. Mario and Pete have gone straight: Theresa's influence. How can I argue with that? And Joseph is making a mess of things.

I guess what I've been looking for is the kind of operation I started with. A few trucks, a few contacts, enough dough to live on. I was a real dummy to forget that things come in a certain order. They start small, advance to medium, and if you've got the smarts, get to large. You can stop anywhere along the line, but you can't go back to the beginning.

And I'm not stopping. Not yet.

Chapter Thirty

~~~

A T FOUR IN THE morning on the next Sunday, Spike ran barking down the stairs from the attic to the window on the stair landing. Lester groaned, sat up and looked at the clock.

"I've got another hour to sleep," he told his dog. "Quit bothering the squirrels." The maples in front of the old rectory had been planted so long ago that their top branches reached the second floor of the building.

Lester knew full well that Spike always had a legitimate reason for barking, so he got up, scuffled into his hard-soled slippers, and the two of them descended the stairs. He unlocked the front door and was ready to step onto the stoop when Spike blocked his way.

The smell hit him first—before he saw the mound of garbage. The sight looked for all the world like a cartoon image. The ground fog made it seem like gray fumes were swirling above the stinky mess. The pile was every color in the rainbow, including a huge dose of red. Lester looked at the oak entry door and saw that it was dripping with red paint.

"Okay, Spike, we're going to call 911—which will be the

first time I've ever called them in this new life I'm living—and then we'll jump over this shit pile and see if there's more at the church. Then we'll call Father Robert." As Lester made the call, Spike stood in place, but his legs quivered and his head hung low.

When the call ended, Lester looked at his dog and knew what was wrong. He didn't bend down or pet him; it would only add to Spike's humiliation for having failed to protect their home.

"Spike. Go!" he ordered.

All of the doors at the church and the parish hall were in the same sorry condition.

Father Robert got there in ten minutes, having run all the way. The police had arrived.

Robert noticed the bored look on their faces that said, "Just another case of vandalism," so he forced them to listen to the details of Nick's murder and the explosion at the food bank, and told them to check with Detective Joyce in the morning. He insisted that they take pictures of all of the five entrances and also the paint-soaked chain-link fence in front of the food bank loading area.

Then he told Lester, "When they're done, we're calling an industrial cleaning service. I don't care if we have to pay them triple time. These church entries are going to be spic and span before the first person shows up for the early service. And I want you here as usual, offering to park their cars and serving your premium coffee."

Lester asked, "Father Robert, do you want me to pretend like it didn't happen?

"Good point, Lester. I definitely will tell the congregation, even if it scares some of them away. Let's leave the side entrance alone so they can see what we're up against."

~~~

ON MONDAY MORNING, JOYCE and Raymond interviewed Ed Grafton a second time. This time Ed's attorney was present.

Once again, Joyce took the direct approach. She pushed the scraps of paper that Mrs. Evans had found in the cash register toward them.

"So you see the three names: Joe, Grafton, and Jones, with arrows connecting them. I know that single names can't count as evidence, but we think that Joe Spano and Mr. Jones are connected to this case, and we think you are too. Believe me, this is Mr. Monte's handwriting; we've had it analyzed three ways to Tuesday. So rather than trying to defend yourself, we'd like you to help us. We're trying to find Joe Spano, and we think you're in a position to help us. That's all we want."

"Or else?" Ed asked, ignoring his attorney's hand signals.

"Or else nothing." said Joyce. "It will just make it harder to find out who murdered Mr. Monte, but we'll get there eventually."

"And just so you know," inserted Officer Chen, "we're looking into your business interests here and in Canada."

"Have a ball," sneered Mr. Grafton. "You won't find anything. And at the risk of being repetitious, I'll say one more time that I didn't know Mr. Monte, I don't know Mr. Spano, and I run a legitimate business. Speaking of fair and square, I'm trying to help the food bank get on solid footing. As a matter of fact, I have a meeting with Father Robert and Terry next week to present a proposal."

～～～

Hi, SWEETHEART, ROBERT TEXTED to Molly the following week. BP today 125/85. MD pleased. Pray it stays down during meeting w/Grafton.

"I have a proposal for you, Father. A good one." Ed Grafton was seated on a couch in the church's library with a reluctant Terry at his side. Robert and his senior warden Lucy Lawrence sat opposite. The glass-doored room with its fireplace, beamed ceiling, and donated Persian rug was the closest thing to a boardroom on the church grounds.

Ed Grafton continued, "I'm looking for a place to relocate my headquarters. I want to be close to the freeway and the port, and the north section of your property fits the bill. The zoning's right and I figure a three- or four-story structure will accommodate me and one or two related businesses. I've told Terry here I'll donate space for his offices, but that the food bank will need to move to a more industrial part of town."

"No," said Robert.

"Who's your backer?" said Lucy, playing good cop.

"That's none of your business, but I wouldn't be here if I didn't have the financing figured out."

Father Robert's foot was tapping at triple speed. "First we have Nick's murder, then an explosion and some serious vandalism. And now you come along with your offer. You must figure we're pretty desperate. What are you planning for the ground floor—a convenience store, or maybe one of those check-cashing places? To repeat what I said earlier … no."

"So you're willing to let that decrepit old house and food bank be a blight on the neighborhood. Hell, all those piles of garbage left on your doorstep were probably spoiled food from Terry's dumpsters."

"No," Robert repeated.

"I agree, no," seconded Lucy.

BP SPIKED DURING MEETING; back down now, Robert texted Molly. Love my new monitor!

Then he called the bishop, who preferred phoning to texting, and told him about Grafton's proposal. This was a tricky call, since his superior was used to being involved in decisions of this magnitude. According to Robert's chancellor—a glorified name for a parishioner who happened to be an attorney—since Grace Church predated the diocese, they could make their own decisions about disposition of church property.

"So who's your chancellor?" the Bishop demanded. "Tell him to call mine and let them hash this out."

Come on, Bishop, do you really want Grace church to share a prime downtown block with a trucking company?"

"I guess not. But next time, do the right thing and call me first."

"Yes, Bishop."

THE NEXT MORNING AT 7:45, Father Robert was walking past the old rectory on his way to work. He patted the phone in his pocket, pleased that it was recording every single step and converting the totals into a graph. He aimed for ten-thousand steps a day. He especially enjoyed Tuesdays, because he conducted an 8 a.m. service in the church's side chapel for a small group of devout parishioners. After giving a short homily, he invited comments. Sometimes their intense discussions continued well into the morning.

He glanced at the space between the rectory and the parish hall at the four-foot-tall concrete cross resting there. It was a Celtic Cross, meaning that a circle was placed in the middle, signifying eternity. Originally the cross had stood on top of the church roof, but an engineer had decided that it was too heavy and likely to topple in an earthquake. So now it rested on the soggy ground, totally out of place. Its main function currently was to provide a place to hide behind for those who needed to relieve themselves, even though the church graciously provided restrooms for all who entered.

Phfft. Phfft.

Robert not only heard the sound, he felt the vibrations before dropping to the ground. He curled up and started to roll toward a nearby rhododendron. Something sharp bit into his hip. He yowled in pain, and then squinted through the branches, hoping to see something or someone associated with the bullets. There were about five people walking on the sidewalk across the street. He slapped the area around his pants pocket, trying to locate his phone, at the same time yelling "Ow! Ow!" as he made contact with the wound in his hip.

A voice in his head said, *Don't faint, not yet.* Robert called 911, and then shouted, "Everyone on the sidewalk; stop!" Of course, everyone within earshot started running.

Robert was soon surrounded by four parishioners arriving for the service. One was a retired nurse, who took his vital signs and ordered everyone to take off their jackets to make him comfortable. The aid car arrived two minutes later, the cruisers right behind. When the food bank line formed fifteen minutes later, the sound of cries and wails rose in the air as the customers realized Father Robert was hurt.

It turned out that the bullets had ricocheted off the cross. A piece of flying concrete, not the bullets themselves, had injured Father Robert.

"I don't think he wanted to hit me, just scare me," Robert told Detective Joyce when she arrived on the scene. "And he succeeded. He also made me as angry as I've ever been in my life. You'll see me down at headquarters after I get patched up."

One of the bullet casings had ended up in a rectory window well. The police later learned that the casing matched the bullets that had killed Nick.

Chapter Thirty-One

Two days later, Father Robert stared up at the dirty ceiling tiles of Detective Joyce's office, waiting for her to come back with the chief. His doctor and Molly had ordered him not to leave the condo for at least forty-eight hours, and Molly had camped out at his place to enforce the restriction. He hadn't minded that at all.

The chief entered the cubicle. Robert stood, and they shook hands. The chief wore a suit and tie; Robert wore a black shirt and clerical collar.

"Father, nobody wishes more than I do that we could catch this guy. I know he's making your life hell, and he's also giving the department a bad name. Just so you know, I was raised Disciples of Christ, so I … well, I think I appreciate what you're going through."

"The denomination doesn't matter," said Robert. "This is a good versus evil problem. And I know that people don't like to hear the word *evil*; it reminds them of Hitler and the devil. But you know," he went on, warming to his subject, "all *evil* means is turning away from the good life—a life that lets you have enough food and water and an education, a life that gives you family and friends, a life that lets you help your neighbors who don't have those things. Sin is evil; selfishness is evil; murder is evil, genocide is evil. Do you agree?"

"Yes, I do," the chief said. "And Father, I'll find the funds to extend the formal investigation, even though we don't have clue one. All I ask is for your 'task force' to stay this side of the law in helping to find out who's responsible for this, uh, evil."

"You know about our task force?" Robert raised his eyebrows.

"Yes, Father. My officers keep me posted. As long as they keep themselves safe and stay well this side of vigilante justice, we welcome their help."

In fact, Father Robert had formed an informal task force, including Lester, Mae, Dr. Lucy, Mrs. Evans, and Arlis. They met weekly to report on their various attempts at investigation. Lester and Mae went door to door in the neighborhood selling cleaning products and watching for anyone suspicious. Lester kept working his contacts under the freeway.

Dr. Lucy mobilized the residents of the retirement homes to keep eyes and ears open while walking their dogs. Arlis kept a close watch from the second-story window of the old rectory.

During her recovery, Mrs. Evans spent many hours doing online research, after accepting Daniel's offer to teach her the ways of the Internet.

After Father Robert's meeting with the chief, Detective Joyce and officer Chen stayed in contact with him and the task force, each of whom appreciated the attention for reasons particular to him or her. For Father Robert, it was essential that this curse be removed from the church property. It helped Lester to stay on the right side of the law. It gave Mae and Mrs. Evans a reason to get up and go out and about each day. It reinforced Dr. Lucy's post-retirement need to serve her church and community. And it brought Arlis slowly out of her shell.

FATHER ROBERT HAD INSISTED that the chief meet with them again in a month. It was now mid-November.

"It's all well and good that you've kept up the extra police patrols," Robert told the chief, "but the Sunday congregation is half the size it was before Nick's murder, even though we provide an escort from the retirement homes and valet service paid for by one of the parishioners. And forget about having an evening meeting or choir practice. They flat out refuse to come." He cleared his throat. "I know I'm venting, but here's the deal. In case it's off your radar, Chief, Christmas Eve is fast approaching. One of the church's major holy days. I guess Jesus, Mary, and Joseph will have to go it alone in a dark manger, inside a dark Grace Church, because people are afraid to attend."

Officer Raymond couldn't resist adding, "I guess it really will be a Silent Night." To cover his unfortunate joke, he went on to say, "Sometimes in a case like this, the bad guy will post a message on social media or call in anonymously, but that hasn't happened here. We haven't had any luck tracking down Mr. Monte's old boss in Canada, and Ed Grafton has an alibi for the time of the murder and the time the shot was fired at you. And remember ... we hit a dead end trying to figure out who was making the threats. It turns out Ms. Perkins doesn't see too well with her drugstore glasses."

"Chief," Robert asked, "Aren't our neighbors in the high rises pestering you about their safety?"

The chief wore a pained expression. "Father, it seems you're too well respected in the neighborhood. We've visited the retirement condo and the public housing tower too. The minute someone starts complaining, the rest shout them down."

FATHER ROBERT ENDED UP relying on Stacy to drum up business for Christmas Eve. They decided against the traditional "Midnight Mass" and moved the service back to 5:30. Stacy put on the full-court press with the news media, and through her contacts arranged for the mayor to attend.

Of course, that meant that the police chief and his brass would be there too. Children and grandchildren were enticed by the promise of a piñata party after the service.

Despite the hullabaloo, the packed church was awestruck by the solemn liturgy, the glorious music, and the singing of "Silent Night" by candlelight. The only glitch occurred when no one could find the statue of baby Jesus for the children's procession to the manger. It turned out that the altar guild had hidden him behind the three wise men and their camel.

THE OFFICIAL VERDICT ON the murder of Dominic Monte was homicide, unsolved. Detective Joyce and Officer Raymond were still working on the case when time allowed.

Stung by Father Robert's refusal to consider his offer to buy part of the church block, Ed Grafton had decided not to cooperate with the police, against the advice of his attorney. Mr. Jones had been extradited to Canada for outstanding warrants.

Raymond Chen wangled an assignment off foot patrol to the department technology unit. He and Joyce met to compare notes on the case every few weeks, since they now worked in the same building. A coin flip determined who sprung for the morning coffee or tea.

Father Robert continued to receive treatment for high blood pressure and the stress resulting from Nick's death, following so soon upon the earlier death in the Memorial Garden. He was fortunate to know a Lutheran minister who was also a psychologist, and met with him weekly. He deepened his friendship with Deacon Mary and her husband Joe, and designated them as his kitchen cabinet, because he was spending so much time at their place

IN EARLY FEBRUARY, AFTER his blood pressure had been normal for two weeks, Robert called Molly. "I'm back on an even keel. Let's have dinner so you can see for yourself."

He would have been thrilled to see the delighted smile on Molly's face.

"Okay, my place at six."

MRS. EVANS, PLEADING ILL health, resigned as manager of the thrift shop, which had been relocated to the basement of the nearby Baptist Church. She also bequeathed her post as altar guild directress to her longtime associate Ginna. At the church's annual meeting, held in mid-February, Father Robert inaugurated the first annual Parishioner of the Year award in Mrs. Evans's name.

After presenting his former thrift-store manager with a bouquet of roses and waiting for the standing ovation to subside, he told the congregation, "This fine lady has known about her honor for a few weeks, because the two of us had to negotiate what would appear on the plaque. I told her in no uncertain terms that naming it the 'Mrs. Evans' Award was a non-starter. After much discussion, she has graciously consented to naming it the Adele Evans Award. Mrs. Evans, would you please say a few words?"

Mrs. Evans stepped forward. She was dressed in tailored slacks and an unstructured multi-colored tweed jacket, selected with the help of Stacy Chase. The frames of her glasses were aqua colored.

"Other than expressing my heartfelt thanks for this honor, which I hope will inspire future efforts to serve the church that we love, I have only ten words to add: *From now on I'd be pleased to be called Adele.*"

TO ED GRAFTON'S EXTREME displeasure, the first floor of the old rectory was now a hangout for people Lester and Mae deemed suitable—meaning no loud voices and no bad smells. It became known as Nick's Place.

Food bank customers and the retired who lived in nearby apartments used Nick's Place during daytime hours to read, play cards, use the donated computers, and pass the time. If someone fell asleep, it was okay, so long as they didn't snore.

In the early evening, a few commuters walking uphill from the downtown offices stopped by, especially if they lived alone and wanted some company. The thrift shop bookshelves remained and were kept full in Nick's honor. A series of trestle tables stretched the length of the former living room, and a circle of comfy chairs filled what had been the dining room. The coffee pot and tea kettle were always on.

The ratio of males to females started at three to zero, but Dr. Lucy and Mae persisted in inviting women and children from the food bank line and the low income housing tower. The former rector's study was now a playroom, and the older ones enjoyed challenging the younger ones at card games, chess, and Scrabble. Friendly animals were also welcome.

Dr. Lucy occasionally gave lectures on oral hygiene, supplying healthy yet delicious treats to ensure good attendance. Mrs. Evans, now reasonably mobile after her stroke, helped with government forms and applications for financial assistance.

Stacy Chase raised funds to install a commercial washer and dryer in the basement and to upgrade the plumbing. The members of Nick's Place now had a place to wash their clothes and take a shower.

Back in good spirits, Stacy was also busy planning the late-March Ash Wednesday Service. The "mainline" churches—Roman Catholic, Episcopalian, Lutheran, and some others—began Lent by reminding the faithful of their mortality. They did this by applying ashes to the faithfuls' foreheads in the shape of a cross, and intoning, "You are dust, and to dust you shall return." It was especially effective as a morning-after tonic for the faithful who had over-indulged during the previous day's Mardi-Gras celebrations.

The mark of the cross stayed on the forehead for many hours, which also served an evangelical purpose: each time someone said, "Your face is dirty," the faithful had to explain why.

Stacy had read about a church in San Francisco that took their Ash Wednesday service to a local park.

"It's like … like a Pop-Up!" she enthused to Father Robert, who decided that the right location for Grace Church to hold the service would be at the north corner of the church block above the food bank entrance. Father Robert and Deacon Mary would offer ashes between 7 and 8 a.m. to the pedestrians coming down the hill to their downtown offices, and then at noon to the food bank customers and residents of the nearby apartments and retirement homes. Sack lunches would be on offer for those who wanted them.

That morning he called together the task force. "I'm sure that Nick's killer is still in the area. Mae feels it too, don't you?"

"I surely do," she said. "Nick has told me so."

"So keep an eye out while we administer the ashes."

AT FIVE MINUTES TO noon on Ash Wednesday, Mae made an announcement to the assembled at Nick's Place. "Get off your behinds and go out there and get your ashes. I'm not letting you back in unless I see that cross on your forehead."

Daniel, who was at Nick's Place working on the sound system, fell into line behind them. He'd tied a bandanna around his unruly hair so that he could present a bare forehead to receive the ashes.

Afterward, he went back to the old rectory to finish installing an easy-to-use console that would allow Nick's Place members to choose from many different styles of music. He would leave it to Lester and Mae to set the rules.

Daniel froze as he re-entered the main room. After listening for a moment, he ran back outside and pulled Deacon Mary away from her duties.

"I heard the sound! It's keys being rattled in the key of G."

Mary paused to process what he'd said. "You mean keys like house keys, right?"

Daniel nodded, forcefully.

"Did you see who was jingling the keys?"

He replied, "I didn't want to yell out like I did when I saw the person who killed Ms. Clare. So I sent up an arrow prayer and then looked to the left, where the sound was."

He paused for about ten seconds.

"Daniel, who was it!" Mary hissed.

"I don't know," Daniel said, "but I can show him to you."

"Thank God Officer Raymond is working at the food bank today," Mary called back, as she ran down the hill.

At that moment, Officer Raymond and Terry were involved in a complex negotiation with a food-bank customer who was insisting he needed ten large bags of rice for his extended family. At Mary's shout, they looked up. She was jumping up and down out on the sidewalk and waving her arms.

"Two, that's all you get," Raymond told the man, and they both went to see what she needed.

"Officer Raymond, Daniel says the person who killed Nick is in the old rectory right now! He says he heard a set of keys jingling in the G key before Nick was murdered and he's hearing the same keys right now!"

Raymond took a breath. This was one of the more preposterous claims he'd heard as a police officer—way more preposterous than a single homeless person demanding ten bags of rice for his family. But nothing was ordinary about this place and these people.

"Let's go." On the way there, he put in a call to Joyce.

Chapter Thirty-Two

DANIEL WAS STANDING ON the street corner beside Father Robert, who said to Officer Chen, "Daniel took me to see the person he heard. It's the same person who asked to speak to me just now when he received his ashes."

"Holy shit!" said Terry. "I don't know anything about the key of G, but there was a guy sitting down my row at Nick's funeral who never stopped jingling his keys. Should I go take a look?"

"Wait until I come out with him," Robert said.

"Father," asked Raymond, "if this is the person who murdered Mr. Monte, and you hear his confession, you won't be able to tell us, will you?"

"No, I won't."

"But," Robert continued, "the part of confession that people don't know about is the desire to repent. So don't be surprised if this man turns himself in. And after talking to Father Whalen in Canada, I'm sure this man is Joe Spano, the head of the criminal syndicate Nick was involved with."

"Is there a place you can take him where he can't escape?" asked Raymond.

"He wants to talk inside the church. My God, man, he's bent

over and limping. Even if he tries to break away, you'll have no trouble getting him."

Raymond answered, "You can limp and shoot a gun at the same time, as he's already demonstrated."

Deacon Mary stepped away and speed-dialed Molly Ferguson's work number.

Robert said, "I'll ask him if he has a weapon. I'll tell him they aren't allowed in church."

Raymond rolled his eyes.

"I'm in civvies, and he doesn't know me," said Joyce, who'd just arrived. I'll go in ahead and hide."

"With all due respect to everyone's sensibilities," said Raymond, "I suggest the most prudent course is to arrest him first and hear his confession later."

"What's our proof if he decides not to confess?" said Joyce. "A set of keys jingling in the key of G?"

"Heard by two separate people at two different times," Raymond reminded her.

A few minutes later, Molly's red Fiat screeched to a stop in the tow-away zone. Robert went to the curb, hugged her as she got out of the car, and they conferred.

"Robert, are you up for this?" asked Molly.

"Yes. I couldn't have said that a month ago, but yes."

"Then go do your job, sweetheart. I'll be here waiting for you."

"CAN I CALL YOU Father, even though you're not Catholic?"

"Yes, Mr. Spano. Our church considers itself … but we won't get into that now. What would you like to discuss?"

"I see you know who I am, so you know what I want to talk about."

"You want to talk about Dom. You know, he was a friend of mine."

Joe Spano said, "I loved him as I loved my own son, but I see now that I failed him. I used him, and so did my associates.

In my world, you accept that you can be used and loved at the same time, but he couldn't." He paused, then continued, "He outgrew me, but I couldn't let go. Probably because my Joe was a disappointment. Then I lost it, and imagined I'd start over here in Seattle without either of them. At age eighty-two. I was giving it a good run until I collapsed on the street a month ago and found out at the hospital I've got only a few months left.

In all his ministry Robert had never talked to someone so unrepentant. He might as well use the opportunity to gain insight into the evil mind.

"Mr. Spano, I know that you come from a Roman Catholic family. I'm sure the players in your game have figured out a way to justify killing someone who betrayed you. And then going to church the next Sunday for your grandchild's baptism. But trying to kill a priest, even a Catholic-light priest like me … how do you figure God will forgive that?"

"That's an easy one, Father," Spano said. "I didn't intend to kill you, just scare you into selling me your property. If I'd wanted to kill you, you'd be dead."

"So why choose to confess to me?" He quickly added, "Not the sin, but the crimes."

"I admire you, Father, that's why. You're stubborn, loyal, and take care of your own."

They talked for a while longer. Then Joe Spano said, "You can come out of hiding, Officer. I'm ready to give a statement."

Chapter Thirty-Three

～～～

A MONTH AFTER JOE Spano confessed to the murder of Dominic Monte, Father Robert was planning the Easter week services. Ten adults and three children would be coming forward for baptism on Easter Eve. The majority were Nick's Place members being sponsored by Lester and Mae.

The happy announcements kept coming. At every Easter service, Father Robert and Molly announced their engagement. They would be married at Grace Church in June.

The first Sunday after Easter, Stacy stood up at the announcement period to say that she was expecting a baby. "And … and … our own Arlis Bell—did you know that her great-grandparents helped my great-grandparents found Seattle?—will be helping me with the planning for Father Robert and Molly's wedding and the other events we have coming up."

Arlis cringed in her pew. Raymond Chen snickered beside her. She'd dared him to come to church, and he'd taken her up on it.

ROBERT FINALLY HAD HIS meeting with the bishop to ask

permission to marry Molly. Combining forces, the two of them requested to be interviewed together, and his superior agreed. The bishop came from behind his huge desk where he perched on a foot-high platform to sit level with them. Robert clutched his notes.

"Molly, you look especially lovely today, and Robert, I don't think I've ever seen you in a suit. Now, since you two are mature adults, and I've seen firsthand that you love each other, I'll just tell you my secret to a successful marriage. It's worked for Betty and me and it will work for you. Every night, the two of you get down on your knees and pray out loud before you go to bed. In our case, we remember our children, and grandchildren, and then broaden out to include everyone in our diocese, our nation, then every believer, no matter what their faith, all over the world. Then we pray for all the forgotten ones, for all of our animal companions and finally for the precious earth and universe that sustain us. That pretty much covers everything, and it puts whatever petty problems we have in perspective."

Robert nodded, imagining Bishop Anthony and his tiny wife kneeling on either side of a double bed in their pajamas. Then he imagined Molly kneeling in a red negligee and blushed to the tips of his ears and top of his bald forehead.

"Put away that list, Robert," the bishop said. "I only have one other question for Molly. What's your last name going to be?"

Molly and Robert looked at each other.

"What if I go by Molly Ferguson Vickers, no hyphen?" Molly proposed.

"I would love that," said Robert.

"Good." The bishop raised his hand. "God bless you both as you enter into a true marriage of heart, mind, body, and spirit."

Molly and Robert hugged each other and cried for a long time, until the Bishop said, "Now let's celebrate with a wee dram of scotch."

～～～

THE NEXT WEDNESDAY, DETECTIVE Joyce and Officer Raymond met in the parish hall with everyone who had helped to solve Nick's murder. Stacy produced leftover bottles of champagne and sparkling cider from the Easter brunch.

For those who hadn't heard, Detective Joyce announced that Joe Spano had died in jail of an apparent heart attack. His family in Vancouver had taken him home for burial.

Lester said, "Now that he's gone to his reward, I sure wish I knew how he got in and out of the old rectory that day."

Officer Raymond replied, "He borrowed a gray uniform like the one most of the service people in Seattle wear. It looks like he went upstairs first and rattled around a few of the water bottles to make it seem like he was making a delivery. Adele Evans told me she saw Tim, the usual guy, make the delivery, but when I followed up with her, she 'fessed up and admitted she just assumed it was him."

Raymond looked over at Arlis, who was tearing up. "Arlis told me right away she hadn't been paying attention. And Arlis, listen to me, it's our bad, not yours, that we didn't figure it out." Mae took Arlis's hand and gave it a squeeze.

"Spano told us he came back down the stairs, bold as you please, turned right into the kitchen, went through the basement door and waited on the stairs. If anyone had confronted him, he'd have said he was a repairman."

"You mean that devil slid by Nick and me without our knowing?" Mae said.

Robert cleared his throat loudly and said, "You mean you and Nick had eyes in the back of your head to notice all two hundred or so people who came in and out of that building on a typical day?"

"Pfft," said Mae. "Maybe that devil got into place when Nick took a break and I was too busy to notice."

"I wonder if maybe Nick *did* see him," said Raymond. "Remember, he wrote the name 'Joe' on the piece of paper we found."

"Mae, how long a break did Nick take?" asked Detective Joyce.

"Oh, about a half an hour. That was long for him."

Joyce coughed, to cover up a little sob. "We'll never know how he used that time."

"What about the other two names on Nick's list?" asked Robert.

Joyce answered, "Ed Grafton finally told us that a few days after Mr. Monte's murder, an anonymous backer contacted him about buying the part of the church block where the old rectory and the food bank sit. It would have been a great investment, given that this area of town is starting to boom again.

"From what we could drag out of him, Grafton planned to build a three- or four-story commercial building with offices for his trucking concern and whatever business his backer was supporting. He claimed not to know if Joe Spano was behind the offer, but did admit it was possible."

Robert was bouncing up and down on his seat. "Just like a year ago when Rick Chase's developer friend wanted to change us into Ye Olde English Amusement Park." Remembering that Rick's wife was in the room, he started to apologize to Stacy.

"Don't worry, Father Robert," she said. "My husband's on the straight and narrow now. He's all involved in making sure the church tower is rebuilt so it will never fall down again."

"But why was Grafton's name on Nick's piece of paper?" Robert asked. "How could Nick have known who he was?"

"Hey!" Officer Raymond raised his hand to get Robert's attention. "Nick was smart. He may have decided that Grafton was just the sort of guy Joe Spano would enlist in his scheme. And remember, Ms. Perkins, you told us how he gave you all the evil eye when you were introduced."

"I surely did," said Mae.

Detective Joyce took up the thread, "As for Mr. Jones, he was a low-level employee in the Spano organization. Spano told us that he brought Jones down from Canada to cause trouble. He started by setting off the bottle rockets at the food bank, and then escalated his tactics to garbage dumping and the other acts of vandalism. Mr. Spano figured he could scare off the church members and force Father Robert into a deal to sell off part of the church block. We'd just sent Mr. Jones back to Canada when Spano decided to use his gun again."

She looked at Officer Raymond, who nodded and said, "Mr. Monte probably had contact with Jones in Canada, and I'll bet Jones came into the building at some point on a scouting mission. Mr. Monte must have figured out that Jones was the guy hanging out at the freeway, in spite of all the confusion about who was making threats against him."

"Argh. Got to stretch." Detective Joyce stood up. Everyone's eyes followed. She regaled them with the yoga warrior pose, first leading with the right foot, and then the left. Her blue blazer strained in all directions, as did her gray slacks.

As she sat down, she continued to give them the lowdown. "We found out where Mr. Spano had been living. He rented a room in that old building right across the street from the food bank entrance, in back of the vacuum repair business. Quite a comedown for someone who ran one of the biggest criminal enterprises in British Columbia. And you know what? We found the weapon in the top drawer of his dresser. He hadn't even bothered to get rid of it."

Arlis, who had listened to the story with hands tightly clasped and brow furrowed, finally spoke up. "How could someone as good as Nick have been involved in a criminal network?" It was almost a cry of anguish.

Father Robert put his hand on her shoulder and said, "Remember, Arlis, he'd changed his ways, and was putting his charming personality to use doing some good. There aren't many of us who don't walk that line between saint and sinner."

"Especially myself," said Lester.

Terry Buffett slapped the table. "Have all the serious questions been asked? Because what I want to know is, Detective Joyce, are you still dating that soccer forward? And if you are, can you break it off, because his game is in the toilet."

Detective Joyce hooted. "We had exactly one half of one date. That guy needs some serious coaching on how to relate to the opposite sex. I almost had to take him down before he wised up."

"One other thing," said Terry. "The thuggish Mr. Grafton actually figured out who'd been stealing from our warehouse, so I guess he has some redeeming qualities. A few small grocers in town couldn't be bothered to go to Costco like everyone else, so they pretended to be picking up product at the warehouse for our satellite food banks. Then they sold it at their places. Now we have everyone wear one of those big ID cards around their neck."

Mae and Deacon Mary, who'd slipped out a few minutes earlier, returned with a big plate of Daniel's favorite oatmeal-chocolate chip cookies.

They raised the plate aloft. "To Daniel," they said.

"To Daniel!" The rest lifted their glasses.

Daniel cast a desperate look at Mary.

"Just say how it made you feel to help find Nick's killer," she suggested.

Daniel stood up. His whole body quivered. "I didn't feel good or bad or anything like that. I just heard a sound one day and then heard it again another day. I don't want any more murders to happen here. That's the prayer I say every morning when I wake up and every night when I go to sleep. Please, God, no more killing."

Lester stood up and hugged him. "Amen, little brother!"

Stacy walked around the circle, refilling glasses. "I couldn't have said it better myself."

Arlis sat up straight and said, "*Ainsi soit-il.*"

"I can say it in Mandarin," said Raymond, and he did.

Terry drummed the table and said, "*Insha'Allah.* It's more 'God willing' than 'So be it,' though. I learned that while traveling in the Middle East."

The others chimed in with variations on the theme, Spike included.

Father Robert, hugging Molly, looked straight up, seeing beyond the thick fir beams of the parish hall. "Nick, remember, you're our guardian. We did our part; now you do yours. Amen, brother."

Photograph by Paul Hannah

KATHIE DEVINY TURNED TO writing after a career as a "government bureaucrat" for Snohomish County, Washington. She has bachelor's and master's degrees in social work.

Death in the Old Rectory is her second Grace Church mystery, following *Death in the Memorial Garden*. Her personal essays have appeared in the *Seattle Times*, *Episcopal Life*, *Cure* magazine and Bernie Siegel's *Faith, Hope and Healing*.

Kathie is married to Paul Collins, an Episcopal priest, who retired as the rector of Trinity Parish in Seattle. She enjoys reading, gardening and volunteering. She especially enjoys bargain hunting at local thrift shops. Paul and Kathie live in Santa Barbara and spend summers near her hometown of Olympia.

You can find Kathie online at Deviny.camelpress.com.

Now read the first book in the
Grace Church Mystery series

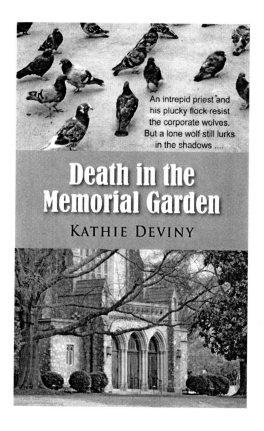

An intrepid priest and
his plucky flock resist
the corporate wolves.
But a lone wolf still lurks
in the shadows ....

Death in the
Memorial Garden

KATHIE DEVINY

A box of unidentified ashes is unearthed during an interment
ceremony. With their congregation dwindling and their
world literally falling in around them, Father Robert Vickers
and his colorful staff members and volunteers put their heads
together to solve the mystery of the ashes and find the means
to save Grace Church from the developers ... all in time for
the Bishop's visit.

Lightning Source UK Ltd.
Milton Keynes UK
UKOW01f0007060216

267813UK00001B/7/P